Praise for Trista Ann Michaels

"Trista Ann Michaels has penned a keeper with *Leave Me Breathless*. It left me completely breathless and yearning for more from this author!"

– Natasha Smith, *Romance Junkies*

"*Leave Me Breathless* delivers it all in this sexually charged novel—strong character, an exhilarating plot, and scorching sex and it all moves at a fast pace. This is a story to seductively seduce the senses of the reader to a pleasurable level of powerful delight."

– Shannon, *The Romance Studio*

"Trista Ann Michaels is a master with words. Her story is absolutely breath taking. There is drama and intrigue and so much more that it is impossible to take a break from the action. This is a must own work of art for any lover of the ménage genre."

– Kimberly Spinney, *eCataromance*

"I thoroughly enjoyed *Leave Me Breathless*, and it may sound cliché, but it did leave me breathless, more than once! I highly recommend this erotic adventure; these two men are worth the ride."

– Stephanie Q. McGrath, *Paranormal Romance*

LooseId®

ISBN 10: 1-59632-876-2
ISBN 13: 978-1-59632-876-1
LEAVE ME BREATHLESS

Originally released in e-book format in November 2008

Cover Art by Anne Cain
Cover Design by April Martinez

Printed in the U.S.A. by
Lightning Source, Inc.
1246 Heil Quaker Blvd
La Vergne TN 37086
www.lightningsource.com

LEAVE ME BREATHLESS

Trista Ann Michaels

Chapter One

Men suck.

Why was it she always ended up with the jerks? The losers? The wimps? What was it about her that attracted them? And why in God's name did she always end up on a date with them?

Picking up the movie ticket that had fallen out of her purse, Tessa Williams stared at it with contempt. Lousy movie—lousy date.

She was a smart woman. She had a master's degree from MIT, for crying out loud. She knew engineering and physics like the back of her hand. It was a shame she didn't know men as well. She fell for it every time—the lines, the come-ons, the sweet talk.

"I know that look," her assistant, Kate, said as she walked into the office.

"What look?" Tessa asked as she dropped the movie ticket into the trash can under her desk.

"The look that says you had another date from hell. Honey, I don't get it." Kate walked around the desk and sat in one of the wing-back chairs facing Tessa. Her purple skirt slid farther up her thigh as she crossed her legs, her matching purple heel dangling off her toe. "You're gorgeous."

Tessa rolled her eyes and pulled a file from the drawer next to her. Kate was the gorgeous one. Her black hair and eyes were the perfect compliment to her deep tan. She got her complexion from her father, a gorgeous Native American who'd worked three jobs to put his daughter through college. Her mother had died when she was eight.

That was one of the reasons Tessa felt so close to her. Tessa had also lost her mother at an early age, leaving her with a father who, at times, had a hard time showing his feelings. He'd been so afraid of losing Tessa as well, he'd become extremely protective. She'd learned to live with it and knew that he loved her, even though he didn't say it as much as she'd like.

"Don't roll those eyes at me," Kate snapped, pulling Tessa from her musings. "You are and you know it. I would kill to have that blonde hair of yours, despite the fact you keep it in the conservative bun on your head. You're smart, powerful."

"Maybe too powerful. Maybe that's what keeps men away. Who wants to be saddled with a civilian scientist for a navy military project and a hard-nosed navy admiral as a father-in-law?"

"You're being silly. You just have bad luck when it comes to men. Stop picking the pansies and go for the hard-asses…literally," Kate added with a nod.

Tessa giggled. "Shawn had a hard ass."

"Yeah, but deep down he was a pansy."

Tessa smiled slightly at the assistant who had quickly become her friend. She was right. Her ex-boyfriend was a pansy. A knock sounded on her office door and Tessa spun her chair around to face it.

"Enter," she yelled out, and a young ensign stuck his head in with a shy smile.

"Morning, ma'am." He spoke in a soft, shy voice and Tessa smiled, trying to put him more at ease. He was new and didn't know her all that well.

"Morning."

He handed her a small wrapped bundle of envelopes. "I have some mail for you."

She reached out and took it from him, her fingers already tugging at the rubber band. "Thank you, Ensign."

"Yes, ma'am," he said with a nod and ducked back out the door.

"Pansy," Kate mouthed silently, and Tessa snorted, tossing a wadded-up piece of paper at her friend. "So what are we doing tonight?" Kate asked.

"You mean besides working late and running through mock launch exercises?" Tessa replied with a grimace.

"Oh, come on. You're not working late again."

"I have to, Kate." With a sigh, Tessa opened the first envelope and stared at the contents.

It was her credit card bill, which showed just how boring her life had become lately. Groceries and gas. How sad was that?

"Tessa," Kate admonished. "You've got to stop working so much and get out more."

"Duh," Tessa grumbled and tossed her billing statement to the desk with a growl of aggravation.

"Why don't you go with me tonight to this new club across town? It'll be fun," Kate teased with a devilish wiggle of her eyebrows, making Tessa laugh.

"I'm sure it would be, but with Admiral Shore in Washington for the week, I have to hold down the fort and make sure these tests run smoothly. He'll have my head if they don't."

"When's he due back?"

"This weekend."

Kate picked up another envelope and slid the letter opener under the flap. The sound of paper separating was the only noise in the quiet room as Tessa thought about how much she'd love to take Kate up on her offer. It had been months since she'd had sex, and the idea of a gorgeous man sinking his thick cock between her legs made her squirm in her leather office chair. *It had been way too long*, she thought with a sigh.

"We'll just postpone the girl's night out until this weekend," Kate said with a shrug and Tessa grinned.

"You're on."

Another knock sounded on the door and Tessa frowned. "More mail, do you think?"

Kate shrugged and moved to open the door. "Director Sparks," she said in surprise.

"Good morning. Is Ms. Williams in?"

"Yes, please come in," Kate replied and stepped aside, allowing the director to enter.

Tessa had met the NCIS director only once, at a formal military function last year, so she was surprised to see him here now. Standing, she moved to greet the director. His tall frame dwarfed hers as he stood in front of her. His no-nonsense stance made her slightly nervous. Light blue eyes scanned the room as though he wanted to look anywhere but directly at her.

"Director Sparks. It's good to see you, but what are you doing here?"

Raising his hand, he ran it through his graying hair and sighed. "I'm sorry, Ms. Williams, but I'm going to need to take you into protective custody. Your father's orders."

"Excuse me?"

"The admiral in charge of the project has disappeared. We suspect foul play."

"Admiral Shore? What does that have to do with me?"

"You're next in command and also the only other person with the launch codes for the new missiles. It's strictly precautionary, I assure you."

Tessa shook her head. "But the codes will be changed, Director. What I have will be useless." Her eyes narrowed as she stared at him. "There's more to this that you're not telling me, isn't there? I want to speak to my father."

"I'm sorry, Tessa. I'll get the message to him, but I'm afraid right now that's not possible. Your safety is what's most important. I have been given authority to take you into custody if necessary."

"Now that certainly sounds like your father," Kate mumbled dryly.

* * *

“What the hell are you doing?” Mitch snapped as he ducked, getting out of the way of a piece of computer memory board flying across the room.

“Sorry. Maybe you’ll learn to knock first,” Jake snarled as he continued to rip apart a CPU.

“What are you? Off your meds again?” Mitch asked with a chuckle.

The lab assistant snickered and Jake shot him a glare, instantly shutting him up.

“What do you want, Mitch? I’m busy.”

“I see that,” Mitch said with a grin.

Grabbing an apple off the counter, Mitch took a bite and slowly chewed as he watched his friend’s anger grow.

“Mitch,” Jake warned, his attention still on the computer. “Either spit it out or get out.”

“Damn, what the hell is gnawing at your ass?”

“Besides you?” Jake snarled.

“He’s been like that all morning,” the young lab assistant said with a shrug. “Not sure what brought it on.”

“I think I know what brought it on,” Mitch replied with a sigh.

Jake’s father had been by to see him this morning, and visits with that man never went well. Scott Bradley was a total jerk, and nothing Jake did pleased him. He’d wanted Jake to go into the military like Mitch had, but Jake had wanted computers. And he was good at them. So good, in fact, NCIS had hired him straight out of MIT as a civilian computer specialist. Mitch had joined up two years later, after he'd been injured on his last SEAL team mission. He couldn't do combat anymore, but he was a damn good investigator.

"I hate to worsen your already foul mood, but the director wants to see us in his office," Mitch said, getting Jake's total attention for the first time since entering the room.

"What about?" Jake asked with a frown.

Mitch shrugged. "Don't know. Maybe it has something to do with that redhead we shared last weekend. You know the one with the big…" He brought his hands up to his chest and held them out several inches with a grin.

Jake shook his head and smiled, despite his mood. "You're a real piece of work, Mitch."

"Yeah, well. At least I'm not the Dom who scared the hell out of her."

Jake scowled. "I did not scare her."

The lab assistant coughed softly, and Mitch turned to look at the young man who had suddenly gone pale. "Just what do the two of you *do* on weekends?" he asked.

"Robbins!" the director's voice boomed over the phone speaker. "I thought I told you I wanted you and Bradley in my office now, not later."

Mitch pushed the intercom button. "Yes, sir, we're on our way."

He glanced at Jake and nodded toward the lab exit door. "We should probably get going, don'tcha think?"

Jake nodded as well and tossed his equipment to the floor as he stood. Glancing toward the lab assistant, he pointed at the CPU. "Don't touch anything."

"Yes, sir," the assistant replied with a wary expression.

Mitch grinned. One thing about Jake—he was definitely dominant. And arrogant. And at times an ass. Hell, *he* should have been the SEAL.

* * *

"Gentlemen," the director said from behind his desk as Jake and Mitch strolled into his office.

Jake cringed. He always hated it when the director started out with "gentlemen." It was never a good thing.

"Director," they both replied in unison.

"I have an assignment for the two of you that's rather unusual."

"So long as it gets grouchy ass here out of the lab, I'm all for it," Mitch said with his usual humor.

The director's lips thinned as he pinned Mitch with his no-nonsense stare. But the former SEAL wasn't daunted. Instead he met his stare, his lips quirking in a slight grin as he dropped into one of the seats flanking the director's desk. Despite their boss's gruff attitude, he actually liked Mitch and knew without a doubt he could rely on him in a pinch.

"What's the assignment, Director?" Jake asked as he took the seat opposite Mitch.

With a sigh, the director ran a hand through his hair. He'd loosened his tie, leaving the first two buttons of his white shirt undone. Something was up, for their boss was never anything but impeccably dressed. There'd only been one other time Jake had seen him this agitated, and it was when Mitch had given himself as a hostage in exchange for a little girl.

The switch had been a brilliant idea, and they'd been able to gain some valuable information, but he'd put himself in an extreme amount of danger, earning a serious butt chewing from the director.

"It appears Admiral Shore has gone missing," the director said, bringing Jake back from his musings with a start.

"You mean the Admiral Shore who's in charge of the new missile project?" Mitch asked.

"That would be the one."

"Has he been kidnapped?" Jake asked.

"Until we hear otherwise, we're running with that assumption. We believe he's been taken for the access codes to the launchers. The only other person who knows those codes is his civilian scientist, second in command of the project."

Mitch shifted in his chair, sitting straighter. "Wait a minute. I don't think I like where this is going."

"Where do you think it's going?" the director asked, a slight hint of amusement in his crinkling eyes.

"Surely you don't want us to babysit this scientist?" Mitch gaped.

"Yes." The director leaned forward and sent Mitch a hard stare. "That's exactly what I want you to do." His gaze shifted to Jake, making him squirm in his seat as well. "Both of you."

"I have to agree with Mitch on this one, Director."

"You may agree with him. It's your prerogative. But you're both overruled. I outrank you. I'm the boss and you do as I say."

Jake gave a quick nod of his head in acknowledgment, but continued on with his argument. "I'm a computer specialist, Director, and Mitch is an investigator. Bodyguards, we're not."

"You are whatever I say you are, Jake. Live with it," the director replied in his usual gruff, brook-no-arguments voice.

"So what are we supposed to do with this guy?" Mitch asked.

"Who said it was a guy?" the director asked, his brow raised.

"Great," Mitch grumbled. "A female scientist."

"What's wrong with female scientists?" the director asked in amusement.

"Nothing," Jake said, pinning Mitch with a narrowed stare. "You can be a real ass sometimes, you know that?"

"Me?" Mitch quipped, pointing to himself. "Come on. I remember school and the smart girls."

"Trust me," the director said, grinning. "You'll be pleasantly surprised. Admiral Williams might not be gorgeous, but his daughter certainly is."

"Excuse me?" Jake choked.

Mitch looked just as shocked. "Are you talking about Tessa Williams?"

"You know her?" the director asked, his gaze shooting back and forth between the two of them.

Jake looked over at Mitch, his chest tightening. Hell yeah, he knew her. In every way possible. He'd thought of her so often over the last two years, wondering where she was, what she was doing. Every woman he'd been with, he'd compared to her.

How did Mitch know her? And how did he feel about the spark of excitement shining in his friend's eyes? He frowned. He didn't like it, he realized. Didn't like it at all.

"I know her. If she's the same Tessa Williams I met in San Diego a few years ago," Mitch said, and Jake's fingers fisted at his side.

Jealousy raced through him as he tried to remind himself this was Mitch. His best friend. They were as close as two men could be, but for some reason, he'd never told Mitch about Tessa. He'd loved Tessa, but had to let her go. Their careers were on different paths. They were headed in different directions. Because of that, he'd kept Tessa a secret, even from Mitch.

The director nodded. "Good. Then things will be easier for her."

Jake wasn't so sure about that. He had a feeling if she'd been with both of them, it would be one of the most uncomfortable times of her life. As well as his.

"Where is she?" Jake asked.

The director inclined his head toward the door to his left. “She’s next door in the conference room. Incredibly irritated. She thinks taking her into custody is uncalled for.”

“Normally it would be,” Mitch agreed. “What makes this case different?”

“Her father, for one. He’s concerned they may go for her next.”

Chapter Two

The door to the director's office opened and Tessa turned to stare at him with a scowl. She hated this. Protective custody? Was her father out of his mind?

"Tessa. I'd like you to meet the two men who will be taking care of you." He waved her into his office. "You should be relieved to find out it appears the three of you know each other."

"What?" Tessa asked as she turned to face the two men. "Oh my God," Tessa whispered as she stared at the two men who had made such an impact on her life.

Mitch and Jake. The two men she'd fallen in love with and then lost. She'd loved them both equally, but separately, and now here they stood together. Jake had been the Dom who'd taught her to let go and allow someone else to be in control. Mitch was the playful rake who'd stolen her heart, but then broken it when he'd chosen his military career over her. She'd understood why, she really had, but that hadn't stopped her from loving him. Even now. Often when her love life went wrong, she would pull out their photos she kept in her wallet and think of them—of what could have been with both of them.

It was more than a little overwhelming, and she clenched her hands by her side to hide the shaking that had started. Did each of them know about her affair with the other?

"Is this going to be a problem?" the director asked as he eyed all three of them with suspicion.

"No," they all said in unison, making the director raise a brow in interest.

"We'll be fine. We were just surprised. Apparently, Mitch and I both know Tessa," Jake said.

Tessa couldn't stop staring at them. Jake with his dark blond hair and deep brown eyes, and Mitch with his black hair and deep blue eyes. They were both so gorgeous and so…God, so muscular. Had they been that big when she first met them? And now that they were both in front of her again, which did she have stronger feelings for?

What am I saying? I shouldn't have feelings for either of them. It's over, has been for years.

Despite that, she still couldn't stop the spread of liquid heat through her limbs as she remembered how things had been with them. Sex with each of them had been incredible, and for a split second, she wondered what it would be like to be with both of them at the same time. The best of both worlds?

"All right," the director said with an unconvinced nod. "Tessa, your assistant packed some clothes for you. I told her to send you an assortment since I don't know where you'll end up."

She glanced over at the two suitcases next to the wall with a sigh. Even with her bodyguards, this wasn't a trip she was looking forward to. "Thank you."

"This will be over soon, Tessa. Mitch, you have the Lear," the director said, and Mitch nodded in acknowledgment. "Jake, you have his back."

"As always," he came back with a grin, and her body warmed in response. Jake had always had such a gorgeous smile.

The director tossed one phone to each of them. "New phones. No GPS tracking. I'm not sure our usual safe houses are a good idea. We're still not sure this isn't an inside job."

"Yes, sir," Mitch said as he studied the tiny flip phone.

Glancing up, he caught Tessa's stare and winked wickedly, making her lips quirk in amusement. Mitch could always make her smile. On the surface, he seemed nutty and comical, but deep down he was all business and took his job seriously. Tessa knew without a doubt she'd be safe in his hands.

As well as thoroughly satisfied.

That thought made her frown, and she glanced toward the window overlooking the Virginia mountains. It was a beautiful spring day. The sun was shining, the birds singing, a cool breeze ruffled the young leaves, but all she could seem to think about was hopping back into bed with her two protectors. The two men she was still half in love with.

"Get going and watch your backs." The director turned to Tessa with a slight grin. "Stay with them at all times and listen to them. Stay safe."

"I will," she said and gave him a small wave as she followed Mitch and Jake out of the office.

* * *

Mitch shifted Tessa's suitcase in his hands as he waited for Jake to load her other case onto the small jet. "How is it you know Tessa?" he asked when Jake stuck his hand out to take the bag from him.

Jake glanced over his shoulder toward the young woman in question as she settled into her seat. "Now's not a good time to talk about this," Jake growled and grabbed the suitcase.

"Fine," Mitch snarled back. "Cockpit, right after takeoff."

Jake frowned and Mitch could see the wheels turning in his friend's mind.

"What's got you so possessive? What difference does it make if I knew her?"

"I know you and she's a gorgeous woman."

"Yeah, so?" Jake shrugged. "Still doesn't explain anything."

Mitch shuffled his feet against the concrete and rolled his eyes toward the cloudless sky. "Remember the woman I told you about who I met in San Diego, but had to leave because we were shipped out?"

"Yeah," Jake groaned, his eyes narrowing.

He nodded his head toward the inside of the plane. "That's her."

"Oh, shit."

"Yep," Mitch said with a sigh. "She's the one that got away."

Jake ran a hand through his hair, and Mitch could tell by his expression and tense body that Tessa had meant something to him as well. But when had they met? Jake had never said anything about her.

"Yeah, we definitely need to talk," Jake said in a quiet voice. "But not here. Later. Where are we going anyway?"

For a second, Mitch glared down at the ground. His mind had been a jumble of goo since he'd seen Tessa standing in that office. "Key West. I…um…made reservations for a beach house under our fake names. Clark. We're brothers and Tessa is"—Mitch frowned slightly—"your wife."

Jake grinned and Mitch wanted desperately to smack his friend. "Not your idea, I take it?"

"No." Mitch placed his hands on his hips with a growl. "Director's idea. He handed me the paperwork and credit cards back in the hangar. We'll explain everything to Tessa in the air. We need to get moving."

Jake nodded and stepped back into the plane, allowing Mitch to enter behind him and head to the cockpit.

Tessa watched Mitch stalk by and wondered at his suddenly almost angry demeanor. "Is everything all right?" she asked Jake as he took the seat beside her.

His heat seeped through her clothes and singed her flesh, bringing sudden images of the two of them tangled together in the midst of soft sheets and limbs.

"Everything's fine. Mitch is..." Jake sighed and buckled his seatbelt. "Mitch is just anxious to be on our way."

She wasn't sure she believed that, but let it go for the time being, and instead chose to study her surroundings. The Lear was gorgeous, with white leather chairs and cherrywood trim. It could hold ten comfortably, maybe twelve to fourteen if they packed them in tight.

"It's a beautiful plane. Where are we headed?"

"Key West," Jake said with a grin. "Do you still love the ocean as much as you used to?"

The question startled her, bringing her mind back to the time she and Jake had spent a weekend at the beach. She had been naked the whole time and completely at his mercy. It was the best weekend of her life. The heat of a blush moved up her cheeks as the memories came flooding back.

"Yes, I still love the ocean," she whispered, then coughed to clear her throat. "What...um...what exactly are we doing? Are we Tessa and Jake, or do we have other names?"

"We are Mr. and Mrs. Clark, and Mitch is my brother. We're in the Keys for a small family get-together."

"So you and I will be sharing a room?"

"Yes. Well, actually we'll be sharing a house. You okay with that?"

Her heart fluttered in her chest at the idea of being close to both of them again. "Yeah, I guess. You?"

She chanced a look at his beautiful amber eyes and swallowed hard at the longing he didn't even try to hide. A longing she felt as well. But she also felt it for Mitch. What the hell was she going to do?

"I'm fine with it. Looking forward to it actually."

* * *

Once airborne, Tessa decided it was time to go talk to Mitch alone. This was turning into an increasingly uncomfortable situation.

"Hey, Mitch. Mind if I join you?"

He turned and glanced at her over his shoulder, his blue eyes sparkling with mischief. "Not at all, Tess. Have a seat." He nodded his head toward the empty first officer's seat, and she squeezed into the tiny space.

"You don't need two pilots to fly this thing?"

"No, not really," he answered with a shrug and adjusted the headphone mic below his chin.

"This is all really weird," she said softly, watching his gaze closely. A shadow passed over his eyes before he quickly covered it up.

"Yeah, seems strange that two best friends who share everything didn't, for some reason, share you."

"Maybe I wasn't important enough to share," she teased, and Mitch snorted.

"I told Jake about you but I never mentioned your name. Jake never said anything at all." His deep blue eyes bored hard into hers, making her body tingle. "I think it was more along the lines that you were *too* important to share. "

"So now what?" she asked, her heart thoroughly confused.

"Well, I figure Jake can have you for three months, then I'll have you for three. We'll just keep rotating you for the rest of our lives." He smiled and Tessa laughed, slapping at his shoulder playfully.

"Very funny." She giggled, but the idea certainly had merit. "Actually, I think I like the idea of sharing you both at the same time myself." She only half meant it, saying it as a joke, but the sudden heated look in Mitch's eyes had her heart pounding out of control.

"Maybe we should discuss this a little further once we're on the ground. Keep talking like that and we'll crash." He wiggled his eyebrows, breaking the suddenly tense and hot mood.

Tessa grinned back in slight relief at his teasing. She shouldn't have said that, but now that she thought about it, maybe it wasn't such a bad idea. She'd never had two men at once before, and she knew them both, so she knew she'd be safe. What better two people to experience a ménage with? It was perfect.

Sort of, she thought as she frowned down at the coastline twenty thousand feet below them. What happened when it came time to choose?

"How did you end up with NCIS?" she asked in curiosity. "The last time I saw you, you were headed to the Middle East."

"I went, was seriously injured, and came back." He smiled slightly and her heart jumped.

"How were you injured? What happened?"

"While on a mission I took six bullets. I don't remember a whole lot of what happened after that. I was pretty drugged up so they could get me out of there. I didn't want a desk job, so I took the partial disability and Jake got me a job here. I guess my degree in criminal psychology paid off," he said with a grin. "Seems I'm pretty good at tracking down the bad guys."

Tessa smiled back. "So why are you babysitting me?"

Mitch shrugged and adjusted the autopilot. "The director thinks there might be a leak somewhere. Admiral Shore's whereabouts, as well as what he was doing, were secrets. He knew he could trust Jake and I, so we got lucky. Although at first, I'll admit to not feeling so lucky. At least until we knew who you were." He turned to her with slightly narrowed eyes. "How come I never knew you were Admiral Williams's daughter?"

"You never asked," she answered, her lips twitching slightly.

"Jake didn't know either."

"Well, Jake probably wouldn't have known who the admiral was at the time. I just…I don't know. I'd gotten to where I didn't advertise who I was much. As you can imagine, the admiral tends to scare people away."

"Not me," Mitch said with a wicked smile. "Not when you were at stake."

She crossed her arms over her chest and shifted in her seat to better face him. "If I recall, you left me. Your job and all."

"I know, Tess," Mitch said. "At the time I thought I was doing the right thing. With me being a SEAL and never knowing if I would make it home or not, it just didn't seem right to do that to you. You deserved someone who would have been there."

"I know," she answered quietly.

She'd understood his argument and at the time had agreed with him. But that hadn't stopped her heart from breaking or the love she felt for him remaining, even after all this time.

"I tried to find you when I got back, but you'd disappeared without a trace."

"I went to work with my father on the missile project in Maryland, then on to Virginia for the final stages with Admiral Shore. It was in Maryland that I met Jake," she added quietly.

Mitch nodded. "It seems strange. Jake and I have shared everything ever since we were younger, even women, but for some reason the thought of sharing you with him…" His blue eyes bored into hers and she shivered. "I don't think I like it."

* * *

"Here we are," Jake said with a sweep of his hand, and Tessa smiled at the beach house.

The white siding, light blue shutters, and gingerbread trim gave it such a charming appearance. A large wraparound porch went all the way across the front, then down the side to the back. The second-story windows were open to the March breeze, which ruffled the white lace curtains.

It was such an adorable place, so peaceful and serene. The sound of ocean waves overrode any street noise as they made their way up the concrete walkway. Impatiens lined the walk and circled the bottom of two palm trees in the yard. Their colors of pink, purple, and white gave the yard a festive flair, and occasionally the wind would catch their scent, sending it her way to enjoy.

"This place is beautiful," she said with a smile.

"Yes, and hopefully safe," Jake said with a smile of his own.

Tessa bit down on her lip as she walked past both of them and stepped into the cottage. She didn't want to believe she was in any real danger. Surely, whoever had the admiral would figure out the launch codes would be changed and that going after her would be a waste of time.

Her high heels clicked on the tile flooring and she quickly kicked them off, letting the cool stone soothe her tired feet. She loved the feel of cool tile beneath her on warm summer days.

"God, I can't wait to hit that beach," she said as she strolled to the massive dining room windows and watched the surf pound against the sand.

"You can go whenever you want, Tess. Just don't go alone," Mitch said from behind her, and she jumped slightly in surprise.

It seemed he could still move around in stealth mode.

"Deal," she answered over her shoulder. "I hope the two of you brought swimming trunks."

Mitch went to put their suitcases upstairs and Jake moved close to whisper in her ear. His hot breath blew against the side of her neck and her whole body tingled in response. She gasped softly as strong, warm fingers came to rest on her ribs, just below her breasts, making her nipples bead and ache. Even after all this time, he could affect her with a simple touch of his hand, a whispered word.

"I think I would prefer to be naked," he whispered suggestively.

"We're too close to the other houses," she mumbled, but the idea had already made her wet with need.

Jake had always liked the hint of danger when he had sex. He enjoyed exhibitionism and the idea that others could see them. If she were honest with herself, she'd admit she liked it, as well. It gave sex such an air of excitement.

He smiled and placed a soft kiss to her temple. "I've missed you, Tessa. I could kick myself for letting you go."

"Our lives were going in different directions. You had your job and I had my promise to my dad to help him with this project."

"He's a smart man keeping you by his side." Jake's finger moved up and ever so slightly brushed the underside of her breasts.

"I'm all he has since Mom died," she whispered, her body leaning closer to his heat, her back arching just a little. "Jake."

"Bags are upstairs," Mitch said as he came barreling down the stairs.

Jake quickly stepped away from Tessa. She stumbled, missing his heat, his warmth, the support of his arms. Afraid to meet Mitch's stare, she grabbed the door frame and fought the heat of a blush as it moved over her cheeks.

"Did I interrupt something?" Mitch stared at the two of them intently, making her feel incredibly guilty.

"I'm going to head upstairs and change," she mumbled and quickly sped past Mitch and up the stairs.

"It's the room at the back, Tess. You have the master," Mitch yelled after her, but he wasn't sure she heard him. With a frown, he turned back to Jake. "We need to talk, Jake."

"I agree." Jake put his hands on his hips and glared across the room at his friend. "I still love her, Mitch."

"So do I."

The two eyed each carefully, neither willing to back down. This wasn't a good thing. Not at all. Mitch had thought of Tessa often over the years, but until he saw her, he hadn't realized just how much he missed her. Now that she was back, he wasn't sure he could let her go again. But what did that mean for him and Jake?

"There's only one thing to do," Mitch said, then let out a heavy sigh. "Let Tessa decide."

"You're joking."

Mitch's lips twitched in wry amusement. "What's the matter? Afraid she'll choose me?"

Jake snorted. "Not likely." He ran a hand through his hair in aggravation and turned to stare out at the ocean.

"We've shared women before, Jake. This should be easy. We both pursue her, seduce her, even sleep with her, and in the end, she decides. Maybe she won't want either one of us."

Jake sighed and ran a hand through his hair again. A movement that was a sure sign he was pissed. He'd be bald if he kept that up. "This is different, Mitch."

"You don't think I know that?" Mitch snapped, then glanced up the stairs to see if Tessa had heard.

With a sigh, he walked over to stand close to Jake so they could talk more quietly.

"I can't believe, as close as we are, we can't do this," Mitch said. "We're like brothers, always have been. We both love her; we both want to make her happy."

Jake rubbed the back of his neck, but kept his gaze on the blue ocean. "So what do we do? Flip a coin to see who fucks her first?"

"That's not funny," Mitch snarled.

"Do you see me laughing?"

"Well," Mitch offered with a shrug. "I dated her first."

"This is ridiculous."

"Do you have a better idea?"

"We should talk to Tessa," Jake said as he narrowed his eyes at Mitch.

"And tell her what? That we both want to make love to her, so which one does she want first?"

"I need to get out of here for a while." Turning, Jake picked up the car keys and headed for the door. "I'm getting groceries; I'll be back later. I've got the cell if you need me."

The door slammed, rattling the windows of the cottage. Damn. He hadn't seen Jake that pissed in years. Mitch stared up toward Tessa's room. She strolled out the door and leaned over the upper railing, her questioning gaze staring down at him. *She's probably wondering what all the commotion was about. What should I tell her?*

"Where's Jake going?" she asked.

Easy question to answer. "Groceries."

"Oh," she said with a nod and pointed over her shoulder to the door behind her. "I'm going to get in the shower."

"All right. Just don't use all the hot water," Mitch teased.

She grinned down at him, making his insides tense. "No promises."

Mitch watched her go and closed his eyes, imaging the warm water cascading down her flesh, her breasts firm and her pink nipples hard, begging him to suckle them. His cock hardened behind his jeans and he tugged, trying to pull the material from his aching bulge. Damn, if he didn't stop thinking about this, he'd come all over himself like some randy teenager.

More than anything he wanted to be in that shower with her, following the water as it flowed down her flesh. Her pussy would be wet, ready for him. Just remembering how tight she had been around his cock had him groaning aloud. She had been such a shy thing, so unsure about her sexuality. He'd loved awakening her to the needs of her body, to the way sex could be.

"Oh, the hell with it," he growled and took the stairs two at a time, heading straight toward Tessa.

Chapter Three

Tessa closed her eyes and let the warm water slide down her tired body. It had been a long flight from Virginia, and she was glad to finally be here. Her room was amazing. The shower was ocean blue tile and big enough for two people. It even had a bench seat at the end, which she'd used to support her foot while she ran her hand slowly down her legs. She'd waxed the other day, thank God, so she hadn't needed to shave.

As she'd surveyed the room and the massive king-sized bed, she'd imagined her and the two hunks downstairs tumbling around in the soft sheets. Could she take both of them at once? The idea was certainly intriguing, but she also remembered how big the two of them were. If it didn't hurt like hell, it would be one fantastic ride.

A noise from the other side of the shower door caught her attention, and she peered through the fog covering the glass door. A shadow moved closer and she tensed, swallowing the desire to yell. It had to be either Mitch or Jake. Why was she so nervous?

The door opened and Mitch stuck his smiling face into the steamy shower.

"Hello, gorgeous. Mind if I join you?"

"What are you doing?" she said with a giggle as she watched his massive body squeeze into the shower that suddenly seemed so much smaller.

His chest was just as wide as she remembered—maybe even more so. He still kept it shaved and she smiled, resisting the urge to run her fingers over his skin and the scars puckering his chest. Moving her gaze lower, she admired his washboard abs and thick, muscular thighs, also covered in puckered scars. She moved her eyes back up to his cock; that glorious cock that had given her so much pleasure in the past. It was massive as it thickened right before her eyes, making her pussy weep with need.

"I thought I'd take a shower, but keep looking at me like that and cleaning will be the last thing on my mind."

"Cleaning was probably the last thing on your mind to begin with," she chastised, but only half meant it.

He smiled and stepped toward her, his heated gaze moving down her body and searing her flesh. She loved the way he looked at her, as though he could eat her alive. He exuded sex appeal, passion, and made her crazy just watching him.

"Where's Jake?" she asked as her heart fluttered wildly in her chest.

"Shopping, remember? God, Tess. You're just as beautiful as I remember."

His fingers followed a trail of water down her arm, sending goose bumps along her limbs and molten heat straight to her core. He could always do that to her. But would he like the body she had now, compared to the one he used to know? And he'd known every inch of it.

"I've put on weight," she argued.

And she had. She'd gone from the size 4 she was when she'd met him to a size 8. Even her breasts had gotten bigger, going from a B to a C. But if the look in his eyes as he stared at them was any indication, he liked the change, and it made warmth spread through her chest.

"It's a hell of an improvement," he whispered and brushed his thumb across her nipple, making it bead painfully. "You're curvier. I like it."

He smiled and her heart practically jumped from her chest. Should she do this?

"Mitch. I don't think this is a good idea. What about—"

"Jake?" Mitch asked, raising an eyebrow.

"Yes, but if he'd approached me like this, I'd be asking what about Mitch," she quickly added, then whispered. "I want both of you."

"Then you'll have both of us, and in the end you'll choose which one you want for forever."

She shook her head in shock, the very idea of having to choose between them making her ill. How could she do that? "No. I can't."

"Can't be with both of us or can't choose?"

"Oh God. You don't know what you're asking."

Her lower lip began to tremble, and Mitch moved forward, cupping her face gently. "Listen to me, Tess. I still love you. I loved you when I left. I've thought about trying to find you so many times. And Jake feels the same way. All we both want is the chance to show you we still love you, and whomever you choose, there'll be no hard feelings. I promise."

"You can't be serious," she whimpered, trying to ignore the heat of his touch and the pressure of his hard cock pressing into her stomach. The look of love in his eyes touched her so deeply. How many times had she daydreamed of him looking at her like that?

"I'm dead serious," he murmured against her lips, making her tremble.

Tenderly, his lips brushed across hers, making her knees weak with need. She wanted this, needed so badly to feel Mitch's tender touch she ached with it. She couldn't think of choosing now. All she could think about was the feel of his hands on her, his lips, his taste.

Mitch slid his tongue past her parting lips to explore her willing mouth, and all inhibitions fled the room. It had been so long, she couldn't stop now even if her life depended on it.

Raising her hands, she rested her palms against his waist then slowly slid them up along his ribs and around his back. His muscles bunched and flexed beneath her touch, making her feel sexy and powerful. He'd always been able to do that. Mitch had been the one to free her of her shy, uncertain shell, turning her into a wild, wanton vixen.

With slight pressure against her waist, Mitch pushed her back, settling them beneath the spray of the rain faucet. The warm drops splattered against them and between them, making her smile. It was like making love in the rain. Now all they needed was a little thunder and the wild, stormy atmosphere would be complete.

The kiss deepened with a moan that rumbled through Mitch's chest, and Tessa answered with a pleasure-filled growl of her own. She loved his minty taste, the way his silky tongue twirled around hers, and she definitely liked the way he sucked at her lips. Everything about the way he touched and kissed sent her senses reeling.

His large palms moved down to cup her breasts and her head dropped back with a sigh. She arched her back, thrusting her breasts farther into his touch, and his fingers tightened, giving her exactly what she wanted.

"Oh, yeah," he murmured as he lowered his head to flick at her nipples with his tongue. "I definitely like these."

She giggled and buried her fingers into his short black hair, holding him closer. His tongue slowly twirled around the tip of her aching mound, deliberately tormenting her before gently engulfing her nipple into his hot mouth. She gasped and her fingers scratched at his scalp. Heat engulfed her as juices poured from her body, sliding down the inside of her thighs along with the water. Her pussy clenched, desperate for the feel of his massive cock filling her to the womb.

Slowly, his kisses worked their way lower. His tongue flicked into her navel, making her lips twitch with a slight smile. Even that little playful touch made her wild. Dropping to his knees, he helped her settle her back against the tile wall, then lifted one leg over his shoulder. Her teeth sank into her lower lip as she waited for the first draw of his tongue along her wet slit. His fingers separated her folds before blowing gently against her clit, making her whole body shudder. Her knees almost buckled as pleasure raced through her veins, sending fire to her loins.

The water continued to create a thick fog around them and roll down her body in sensuous rivers of delight that only added to her arousal. Sex in a shower was so amazing and wild. Especially with Mitch.

Two fingers slid into her depths, teasing her without mercy as he slowly fucked her with his fingers. His warm tongue circled her clit with deliberate intent, making her whimper in building need. Her pussy convulsed around his fingers, trying to pull them deeper, but he kept them shallow. He purposely drove her insane, made her so desperate she could beg.

"Mitch," she groaned and wiggled her hips against his face, looking for a firmer touch.

"You taste so good, Tess. Just like I remember," he whispered before continuing the slow licks of his soft tongue.

He turned his fingers, curving them to hit her G-spot, and she bucked her hips wildly. The beginning stirrings of her climax raced through her, making her gasp and claw at his head with desperation. Oh God. If he pulled back now, she'd die. She was so close her whole body trembled.

"Oh my God." She gasped and would have fallen if her back hadn't been supported by the cool tile.

Every nerve ending in her body erupted into a massive ball of fire as pulse after pulse raced through her pussy. Mitch fucked her hard with his fingers, pushing them deep, increasing her pleasure. The pulses shook her body, and her stomach jerked with every earth-shattering clench of her vaginal walls.

Mitch continued to lick his fill and soothe her with his fingers as she slowly floated back down from her intense physical high. That was exactly what she needed, but even as incredible as it had been she wanted more. She wanted his cock buried deep inside her.

"Mitch. I still need you," she whispered, her hands trying to tug him to his feet.

With a groan, Mitch stood and pulled her with him to the bench. He sat, then turned her so her back faced him before settling her on his throbbing cock.

"Take me inside you, Tess," he whispered as his cock gently slid along the cleft of her ass.

A wicked smile crossed her lips as she began to move with him, teasing him like he'd teased her. He moved his knees between her thighs, spreading her legs wider.

"Damn it, Tess. You're killing me."

His hands gripped her waist and lifted her, settling the head of his thick cock at her soppy opening. She was just as wet as before, just as desperate for the feel of him moving inside her hungry pussy. With a growl, he pulled her down, thrusting his cock balls deep. She panted and began to move, letting him come almost all the way out before slowly sliding back down his length.

His hands slid around to cup her breasts. He squeezed them before pinching her nipples between his thumb and forefinger. The slight bite of pain made her chest rise on a sharp intake of breath, shooting sparks of pleasure all through her. His thick cock stretched her, filled her, and she began to increase her movement, fucking him harder and faster.

Without warning, he pulled from her pussy and moved his cream-covered cock to the tight hole of her anus. She was practically panting now, desperate for him to take her there. It had been so long since she'd felt him inside her ass, felt him dominating her.

"Do it," she whispered.

Gently, he surged forward, past the tight ring of resistance, filling her ass completely. The pain only intensified her pleasure, and she let her head drop back to rest on his shoulder. His teeth nipped at the side of her neck and she moaned in total rapture. Could it get any better than this? Farther he slid into her, filling her even more, and she rocked against him, silently begging him to give her everything he had.

His hand took hers and moved it to her pussy. She could feel her heat and her juices as her fingers began to play with her slit. They brushed across her clit and she gasped, bucking her hips toward her hand. Mitch groaned and his body tensed behind her. He was as close as she was. Reaching between her legs, she cupped his tight balls, massaging them.

"Oh, fuck yeah, Tess," he murmured, then gripped her hand, moving it back to her pussy. "Fuck yourself with your fingers while I fill your ass. Make yourself come for me."

She slid two fingers deep into her vagina, and her eyes rolled back into her head at the searing pleasure that sped through her. It felt so good. She could feel his cock moving against her fingers through the thin membrane, and she rubbed against him, adding to his pleasure, as well. They moved against one another wildly, their bodies melding together perfectly.

The same tingling heat she'd felt before raced through her with a vengeance, stronger and more intense. Her ass muscles clenched around his cock, making Mitch gasp in pleasure. Juices coated her hand as her fingers pumped harder, matching the rhythm of Mitch's movements.

"Fuck, Tess."

He added his touch to her clit and she exploded amidst blinding light and scorching rapture. Everything seemed to go white as she rode out the waves of her release, Mitch pounding into her over and over. Seconds later, Mitch tensed as his hot seed emptied deep within her ass.

"Wow," she sighed and sagged against his chest.

"Oh, hell yeah," he grumbled into her neck and she giggled. "I guess I should have brought a condom."

"It turned out you didn't need it. But don't worry. I'm on the Pill."

Mitch smiled and kissed her cheek softly, his cock going slack in her ass. "We should probably get cleaned up before we lose the hot water."

With a reluctant sigh, Mitch helped her to stand. Her legs shook and she gripped his strong arms, holding herself steady. Beneath the warm spray of the water, they cleaned each other off between gentle, teasing touches and soft kisses. It felt like old times again, and it was the happiest she could remember being in a while.

The only thing that gave her pause was Jake—and how much she wanted him as well.

* * *

Tessa stood knee-deep in the surf, watching the seagulls fly overhead. The cool ocean water lapped at her thighs and the sand shifted beneath her feet. As her gaze moved to the star-studded horizon, she tried to fight off the guilt she felt eating at her insides.

When Jake had first returned with the groceries, she'd had a hard time looking him in the eyes. Did he know what she and Mitch had done? And did it bother him? His narrowed gaze toward Mitch when Jake had first noticed her nervous attitude made her think it did.

This idea of Mitch's was insane. Wasn't it? She loved them both. Always had. How could she possibly choose? She'd enjoyed sex with Mitch and had no doubt sex with Jake would be just as incredible, but was it right for her to do this? What would this do to Mitch and Jake's friendship?

With a growl of aggravation, she piled her hair on her head and let the breeze cool her heated neck. It was a shame the wind couldn't whisper the answers to all her problems. She certainly couldn't talk with her father about this. He was conservative, stuffy. He would never understand. Even as close as they were, she'd never been able to talk about relationships and sex with him. Besides, what father would want to know his daughter was sleeping with two men at once so she could decide which one she wanted forever?

I've gotten myself in one hell of a mess, haven't I?

"Weren't you told not to come out here alone?"

Jake's deep voice startled her and she began to turn, but his hand on her upper arm held her in place. Her heart pounded furiously in her chest. Would he punish her? Jake's punishments were almost as good as sex itself, and more than once she'd come just from the spankings alone. There had been numerous times she'd done something deliberately just so he would punish her. Jake knew it. He seemed to enjoy the punishments almost as much as she did.

"I'm sorry. I forgot. I'm not used to having to report to someone," she whispered, her gaze locked on the bright sliver of the thumbnail moon. She let go of her hair, letting it cascade down her back.

"This is serious, Tessa. Please treat it as such. I don't want anything to happen to you," he added in a low whisper against the side of her neck, and tingles of desire ran down her spine.

"I don't want anything to happen to me either," she whispered back.

"I think to ensure you won't do it again…you should be punished."

His hand slowly skimmed down her shoulder blades to the hook that held the top of her bathing suit closed. A simple flick of his wrist made it pop open, and she reached up with a gasp to hold the flimsy material to her chest.

"Jake," she started, then flinched in a mixture of pleasure and pain when he slapped her ass.

"Are you questioning me?" his voice rumbled, but she didn't miss the slight hint of amusement in his deep tone.

"No." She shook her head, her body heating in anticipation of what his punishment might be.

It didn't surprise her he would do it here in the open. Jake enjoyed the slight danger of exhibitionism. And even though she was loath to admit it, she did too. The beach was deserted, but could the people in the other houses see them from inside? Would they step out onto their decks and watch them have sex in the surf? The very idea sent her pulse pounding through her ears in excitement.

"Let the top go," he murmured as he tugged at the string behind her neck.

She did as he instructed, letting him toss the material back to the beach. The cool night air hit her nipples and they beaded instantly, anxious for Jake's hot touch.

"Now the bottoms," he instructed, and she quickly pushed them down her legs so that he could toss them to the sand as well.

His hands explored her naked back, his soft touch sending shots of pleasure straight to her aching core. What happened to the punishment? Or was this the punishment? To drive her crazy with need? Slowly, his fingers slid along the cleft of her ass and circled the tight hole of her anus, making her shiver in excitement.

"It's been a long time since I've felt the heat of your ass around my cock," he whispered, gently teasing the puckered hole with the tip of his finger.

Every nerve ending in her body screamed as intense heat raced through her. Her juices slid down the inside of her thighs and she squirmed against his touch, desperate for more. It was amazing how fast he could have her panting.

"Maybe this should be your punishment. To tease you until you beg for it."

"I'm close to begging already," she whispered, then gasped as his free hand slid around to pinch at her hard nipples, rolling them between his thumb and forefinger.

He slapped his palm across her ass, the sting only adding to her pleasure, and he did it again, this time rewarding the other side. With a gasp, she bent forward slightly, silently asking for another.

He chuckled and bent down to softly kiss the stinging flesh. "You always did like being spanked, didn't you?" he purred as he turned her to face him.

His tongue flicked out to lick her belly button, and she closed her eyes as pleasure tightened the muscles of her body.

"Not much of a punishment if you enjoy it," he purred and worked his way upward toward her breasts. "But at the moment, I've been without you too long. I think I want to fuck you instead of punish you."

His mouth closed over an aching breast and she moaned loudly, not caring who heard. Her fingers buried in his thick, dark blond hair and tugged him closer. His mouth was hot and wicked as he suckled her harder, making her pussy throb and convulse.

Sitting back onto the sandy bottom of the surf, he tugged Tessa down onto his lap. His wide, smooth chest appeared to shine in the soft moonlight and she gently ran her fingers along his flesh. His cock pressed against her aching pussy and she wiggled her hips, rubbing the head of his thick shaft along her slit.

She loved the feel of his cock. It was like steel covered with a thick layer of velvet that could make her scream in pleasure as it filled her to the point of tearing. His stare bored into hers like hot flames and she couldn't turn away as his lips descended hungrily onto hers. He tasted of wine and pizza. Sweet and spicy all rolled into one, and she slid her tongue past his lips to get more of his alluring taste. The ocean waves pushed and pulled at their bodies as they crashed against the sand, rocking them against one another in a rhythm that ignited their desire even more.

Lifting her hips, she slid down his length, taking all his thick girth into her waiting body. Her head fell back with a moan as she pushed down harder, taking even more of him. He groaned and bit at the side of her neck, his teeth scraping along her skin. Sharp shots of pleasure vibrated through her limbs in a frenzy of tingling prickles.

He felt so good, but it was too slow. She needed it harder, faster. She wanted him to pound into her with his usual force and demanding control. Climbing off him, she ignored his questioning glance as she waded close to shore, then dropped to her knees.

"Fuck me, Jake," she ordered over her shoulder. "Fuck me hard."

A tiny smile lifted the corners of Jake's lips as he stood to do her bidding. But not before he had a little fun first. Going on his knees behind her, he gave her shoulders a gentle shove, encouraging her to rest on her hands. His other palm slid around the globes of her tight ass. The moonlight made the water droplets sparkle like diamonds against her tan skin and he smiled as his fingers slid along the cleft of her wet ass.

She moaned and moved back as he inserted two fingers into her dripping pussy, wetting them with her juices.

"You're so wet, Tessa," he purred, then slid his fingers to the tight hole of her anus. "Do you want them here?"

"Yes," she groaned.

He pushed them knuckle deep and she sighed, slamming her hips back against him. His cock jerked, wanting desperately to be back inside her willing body, but not yet. He wanted her begging.

"Does that feel good, Tessa?" he asked as his teeth nipped at her hip.

She groaned an answer and he stood straight, then slapped at her hip hard, making her gasp.

"Answer me, Tessa," he ordered.

"Yes," she said with a sigh. "Yes, I like it."

"Good girl," he purred and pushed his fingers a little deeper, slowly fucking her ass. "What else do you want, Tessa?"

"Spank me again," she said, then gasped as though surprised she'd said it.

Jake smiled, then slapped her hip again. She moaned and pushed against him harder. She was killing him. The intent had been to make her beg, not make himself lose control, but damned if he wasn't close. It had always been like that with her. Even though he was the Dom, she always seemed to be the one in command.

"Please, Jake," she whimpered and dropped her head toward the water, sticking her ass higher in the air. "I need you."

"Where, Tessa?" he demanded.

"Everywhere," she screamed and brushed her thick mane from her face, sending him a heated look over her shoulder.

He settled the head of his shaft at the opening of her pussy while keeping his fingers deep in her ass. "I don't have a condom, Tessa," he grumbled.

"It's okay. I'm on the Pill," she groaned and pressed back against him. "Please, Jake."

Jake stalled. "I've never had sex without a condom."

She glanced at him over her shoulder. "What?"

He shook his head and pressed the tip of his shaft into her pussy. She sighed, pressing back and taking him deeper, forcing him to fill her. Her heat engulfed him, seared him as he slid balls deep. His own growl of pleasure startled the seagulls on shore and they flew away, leaving just the two of them moving with the waves of the ocean. The water lapped at their legs and shifted the sand beneath them, making it hard for him to keep his knees steady.

Her wet pussy squeezed at his cock while her ass squeezed at his fingers. She was so tight and hot, so perfect he wasn't sure how much more he could take. How much longer he could go before exploding.

Every part of him tingled with an oncoming release so strong he wanted to shout. It took everything he had to hold back, to allow her to find her pleasure first. Her hips rocked against him as he moved his cock and fingers together, rubbing against that special spot he knew would send her reeling. They pounded against each other harder, their rhythm becoming almost frantic in their need to find release.

The walls of her pussy rippled along his length and he growled deep in his chest as though trying to hold on to his soul. She felt so damn good.

"Jake, please. I need to come," she begged.

"Yes, baby," he purred. "Come for me."

Instantly she exploded, her pussy and ass squeezing him to the point of pain, and he pushed even deeper, spilling his seed into her body as his own erupted into a massive ball of rapture. Everything around him blurred except for the feel of her body pulsing around his.

Chapter Four

Tessa sighed as Jake laid her in the bed and covered her quivering body with a blanket. His amber eyes held just a hint of sadness and uncertainty as he brushed the hair from her eyes with a gentle touch. It hurt her to see him like that, his normal confidence diminished.

"Jake," she whispered, her voice almost breaking on a quiet sob. "Are you sure this is a good idea?"

He placed a single finger across her lips and smiled. "I'll take you any way I can get you. Even if I have to share you with Mitch."

"But what if I..." She swallowed, unable to even form the question for fear of hurting him.

"What if you choose Mitch?" he asked, his lips twitching slightly.

She nodded and licked her dry lips as his thumb brushed away a single tear from her cheek. "Yes."

"Don't cry, Tessa. Whoever you choose, it'll be okay."

"But I can't be what comes between you and Mitch. You've been friends too long."

"And that's why we'll still be friends, no matter what the outcome. We're half of the same whole. Have been our entire lives. I guess it's only natural we both love you. And we'll both probably always love you. So don't let this upset you, Tessa. Just let things happen as they may."

She nodded and closed her eyes, letting Jake's fingers comb a soothing path through her hair.

Once she was asleep, Jake stood and headed downstairs to help Mitch finish securing the house. He was surprised to see his friend sitting on the sofa, his attention glued to the news.

"Finished securing the perimeter?" Jake asked as he headed to the small kitchen to grab a soda.

"Yeah," he answered, but kept his gaze on the screen.

"That was fast."

"Ex-SEAL," Mitch answered, as if that was all the answer he needed.

Jake snickered, then took a close look at the pinched and tense expression on his friend's face. Maybe this thing with Tessa was affecting them more than they wanted to admit to one another.

"Tess asleep?" Mitch asked, then raised his hand to take a sip of his soda.

"Yeah, although I'm sure it won't be a peaceful sleep. She's too uptight." Jake paused, trying to decide how to broach the subject of Tessa. "Mitch," Jake started with a sigh.

Mitch held up his hand, stopping Jake from saying anything more. "Don't."

Taking a seat in the small chair opposite the couch, Jake leaned forward and rested his elbows on his knees. "We've shared women all our lives; why is this so hard?"

"Because we both love her."

"Then maybe we should do this together as opposed to separately. If we're both there…like we normally are…then maybe it'll be different."

"And maybe it will be harder."

"Damn it," Jake snapped and stood. "It's got to be better than one of us sitting down here while the other fucks her upstairs."

Running a hand through his hair, he paced the small room before glancing down at Mitch. His friend watched him with a mixture of amusement and apprehension.

"Why didn't you ever tell me about Tessa?" Mitch asked, throwing him off guard.

"I don't know," Jake said with a sigh. "I guess…she was the first thing that had truly been mine. The first woman I had feelings for who I didn't share with you." Jake's lips spread into a wry smile. "Or at least, so I thought."

"You met her about two years after me. At the time, I was six months into physical rehab and trying to find her."

"You never told me her name," Jake said.

"Yeah, I know. And my guess is for the same reasons you had. Small world, huh? That we would both end up falling for the same woman, but at different times."

"Yeah." Jake dropped back down into the chair and let out a huff of air. "What if she picks me?"

Mitch shrugged, then glanced back at the television. "I'll still be your friend, just don't expect me over for Christmas for a while. At least you'll know if anything happens to you, she'll be taken care of."

Jake pursed his lips with a frown. An idea began to form in his mind, but it was so outlandish, he refused to think it through. They would be locked away, for what he had been thinking was illegal.

* * *

Admiral Williams continued to go over his notes. He was missing something. He had a bad feeling about all this and was glad Director Sparks had gotten his daughter to safety. He really didn't think they would go after her, but he wanted to be on the safe side.

Something about Sparks made him nervous, but he couldn't quite put his finger on what. There were too many numbers that didn't add up, too many questions without answers.

A knock sounded at his door, breaking his thoughts. "Enter," he replied, and set his notes aside.

His assistant stepped into the room and softly shut the door behind him. Admiral Williams waited patiently as his assistant came forward. He stopped just in front of his desk, his hands clasped in front of him.

"Captain Neese called. They found Admiral Shore's body just a few miles outside D.C."

"Murder?" Williams asked.

"That's not been determined yet, but I got the impression they're leaning in that direction."

Williams sighed and leaned back in his chair, his gaze focused on a spot over his assistant's right shoulder.

"You don't seem surprised."

"I'm not," Williams admitted. "Even if he'd talked, they couldn't let him live. He would have been able to identify them."

"Do you still think there's someone on the inside?"

He nodded his head. "Yes. Now I just need to figure out who it is."

* * *

Tessa strolled down the stairs, a light blue sundress over a matching swimsuit her chosen attire for the day. She hadn't been to the beach since she and Jake had dated. She was anxious to spend the day sunbathing and swimming in the warm water of the Keys.

Jake and Mitch were already downstairs. She'd smelled the coffee and bacon all the way in her room, and had quickly piled her blonde hair on her head and dabbed on a little makeup so she could join them. She stood at the bottom of the stairs, her hand resting on the column, and watched the two of them.

Jake stood at the stove cooking. His beige Dockers hugged his hips and accentuated his slim waist, making her mouth water. The light blue polo shirt made his tan and dark blond hair stand out, and for a second she remembered how those thick locks had felt between her fingers.

Her gaze moved to Mitch, who sat at the breakfast bar glancing through the paper and sipping coffee. His short, cropped black hair looked just like it always did, perfect. His black lashes lay against chiseled cheeks as he continued to study the paper. Glancing down, she noticed his bare feet and smiled. Jeans, T-shirts, and bare feet—that was Mitch, whereas Jake was more the preppy type. Always clean-cut and immaculately dressed.

With a grin, she inhaled the scent of Jamaican Blue Mountain coffee. That was Jake's coffee of choice and, even though it was expensive, it's what he always drank. With a frown, she wondered where he'd found it or if he had brought it with him from home? Neither seemed to notice she was there yet as they talked quietly about what was in the paper.

Clearing her throat, she caught their attention.

"Morning, beautiful," Mitch said with a wink over his paper.

"Morning, Tessa," Jake said with a smile and she grinned back, thoroughly enjoying waking up and finding both of them in her kitchen.

"Morning. What's for breakfast?" She walked over and sniffed at the bacon frying in the skillet. Next to it was a skillet of potatoes with a hint of garlic.

"The works," Jake said and placed a light kiss on her cheek. "Sleep okay?"

"I suppose. I always have a hard time sleeping in a strange bed."

"I remember," Mitch said with amusement as he slid a cup of coffee across the counter for her.

Jake gave him a strange look over his shoulder before turning back to the food. It wasn't like Jake to be jealous, and it bothered her to think she might be hurting him. She would rather be without them than to hurt either of them.

"I hope you're hungry. I made a lot," Jake said and set the skillet full of bacon aside.

"I'm starving."

Strolling over to the breakfast bar, she took the stool next to Mitch and began to read his discarded sections of the paper. Her cell phone beeped, making her jump, and she quickly ran across the room to grab it.

"What the hell was that?" Mitch asked, laughing at the unusual, high-pitched sound.

"My cell. I just got a text message." She flipped her phone open and read the message.

Shore dead. Inside man. Watch your back, Bella.

"Oh my God. It's from Dad. He says Shore is dead." She stared at the phone in shock, her hand shaking slightly. She didn't know Shore all that well, had only been working with him for a year or so, but the idea he was dead still made her sad.

She sniffed and wiped at her nose. "What does he mean by inside man?" And what did he mean by "watch her back?" Did he suspect Mitch and Jake? That was crazy. They would never do anything like that. They would never work for criminals.

"Director Sparks mentioned the same thing. His schedule and whereabouts were top secret, so there has to be someone on the inside who got the kidnappers that information. You okay?" Mitch asked, and he raised a hand to rub her back.

She nodded, again sniffing back tears. "Yeah. I'm fine." Without another word, she closed her phone.

* * *

“Have you gotten her whereabouts yet?”

Scott looked up from the GPS tracker and nodded toward the young Korean, Jin. “She’s in the Keys.”

“What about the admiral?”

“Her father?” Scott asked, his brow raised. “He’s snoop-ng around, but he won’t find anything, so don’t worry about him.”

“What if he does? Find something, I mean.”

Scott glanced down at the GPS signal on his laptop. “Then we use his daughter to keep him quiet.”

Chapter Five

After breakfast, Jake and Mitch took Tessa out to the beach to try to get her mind off everything that had happened over the last couple of days. But Tessa was a strong woman and it didn't take her long to relax. She laughed, enjoying the warm March sunshine. She lay on the sand, her bikini top undone so her back could tan without lines. Her thick hair was piled on her head, exposing her slim neck.

With a smile, Jake remembered the first time he'd met her. She was so frazzled, she thought he was the copy machine repairman and actually snapped his head off for taking his sweet time in getting there. When he'd pointed out her mistake, she'd blushed a deep pink, and he thought she was so adorable he'd fixed the copier despite her surly disposition.

Turns out she had a right to be slightly perturbed. The tiny blonde was the civilian in charge of the military project. The missile engineer he'd just been hired to set up the computer networking for. The poor woman couldn't seem to get a minute to herself before someone was asking a question or screaming for help. She easily—if somewhat raggedly—did the job of three people.

He realized she needed a break. Not just physically, but emotionally. And that's how their relationship had started. Unfortunately, it had ended before he'd been able to tell her how he felt. Well, if he were honest, he wasn't even sure how he'd felt at the time. It was after they'd been separated for a few weeks that he realized he was in love with her and had done the most stupid thing of his life.

Could he let her go again if she chose Mitch?

Speaking of my friend, he thought with a frown as he watched Mitch slowly approach Tessa with a large glass of seawater.

Jake opened his mouth to stop him, but Mitch put his finger in front of his lips, silencing him. Relaxing back in the beach chair close to Tessa, Jake waited for the show as Mitch dumped the cold water onto Tessa's back.

"Oh my God!" she screamed and sat up, shooting daggers in Jake's direction.

"It wasn't me," Jake said with a chuckle.

"You couldn't warn me?"

"Wait a minute." Jake snorted with amusement. She hadn't yet remembered her exposed chest and he took his time reminding her. He enjoyed the view of her perfectly rounded globes and pink, perky nipples. "Mitch dumps water on you and I'm the one who gets yelled at?"

"Sounds good to me," Mitch drawled.

With a growl, she turned and tossed her towel at Mitch, who dodged it with a laugh. "Surely you can do better than that, especially seeing as you don't have a top to hinder you."

Tessa gasped and glanced down at her chest. Jake couldn't help but laugh out loud at her completely shocked expression. Her hands rose to cover herself as she frantically searched the beach for her top. Feeling devilish, he held it out to her, dangling it from the tip of his finger.

"Looking for this?"

She reached out to take it from him, but he snatched it back. "Eh," he chided. "Not until you make it up to me."

"Make it up to you?" she asked, her mouth gaped open in outrage.

"Yes."

Jake's lips spread into a sexy grin, and Tessa's whole body heated. He was so gorgeous when he was being playful, but it was daylight and there were other people on the beach. She couldn't be out here without her top. Someone would call the cops and have her arrested for indecent exposure.

"Come on, Jake," she said, her gaze glancing around the beach. "Someone will see me."

"Then you better hurry," he said with a grin.

Tessa sighed and scooted on her knees next to his chair. "What do you want?" she asked in exasperation.

"Well, with that attitude…" he chided, and stuck her top in his pocket.

With a growl, she narrowed her eyes. She could hear Mitch chuckling behind her and she turned to glare at him as well. "Thanks for helping."

"Don't mention it," he teased with a wink, those sexy blue eyes of his crinkling at the corners.

Her heart raced wildly at the heat emanating from his gaze. Two could play at this game. With a wicked grin, she turned back to Jake and softly circled her nipples with her fingers. His eyes moved to her chest, watching every movement of her fingers. His gaze darted back to hers, the darkening chocolate orbs making her flesh tingle. Using the tip of her tongue, she wet her lips enticingly and watched as the bulge between his legs grew.

"I'm sorry, Jake," she purred. "Do you forgive me?"

"Maybe."

"If you spanked me, would that make it better?"

"Ah, hell," Jake mumbled and Tessa bit back a laugh, even though she could feel herself getting wet just thinking about him slapping her ass with the palm of his hand.

A smile curved Jake's lips as he reached forward to grab her hand. "I think I have a better idea."

"What?" Tessa asked with a grin.

Without answering her question, Jake spun her around and made her face Mitch. Strong fingers held her hands imprisoned behind her back, thrusting her breasts out farther. Jake's sexy voice rumbled in her ear, making the very core of her melt into liquid heat.

"Come here, Mitch," Jake ordered, and Mitch moved forward to kneel in front of her, blocking her exposed chest from the other people on the beach. "Kiss him, Tessa."

His order startled her, and for what seemed like endless seconds, she and Mitch stared at one another. Both seemed to be just as uncertain as the other.

"Our neighbors will think we're crazy," she whispered as Mitch brushed a windblown lock from her cheek.

"Don't worry about what they think, Tessa. Kiss him."

Mitch waited silently for her to make the first move, to initiate the kiss. She desperately wanted to, but it felt so odd doing it here in front of Jake. They both loved her and wanted her. Would it be awkward or natural?

"I want you to do it, Tessa. I want you to kiss him. In front of me. In front of everyone. Do it," Jake ordered.

She leaned forward without a second thought, obeying his commands just like she always had in the past.

Mitch's lips were soft against hers. And warm. They were always so warm. Her tongue licked at his lower lip, toying with his full, delectable mouth. Mitch's kisses were so different from Jake's. They were gentle and slow…unhurried and so incredibly sexy. She loved the way he kissed and parted her lips in invitation. His breath was warm and minty as it blew enticingly across her mouth with his softly spoken words.

"You're supposed to kiss *me*, Tess. So kiss me," he murmured, his voice vibrating through her entire body.

Blood flowed hot and fast through her veins as she slid her tongue past his parted lips and tangled with his. A deep moan penetrated her foggy brain and she realized with surprise it was hers. Her nipples tingled and beaded painfully as Mitch flicked his thumb across her aching buds before deepening the kiss and practically devouring her.

Jake's fingers continued to keep her hands pinned behind her. Twice she tried to break free to bury her fingers into Mitch's hair, but Jake held her tight, his lips softly nibbling at her shoulder. His other hand moved around and cupped a breast. Long fingers pinched at her nipple, and she gasped into Mitch's mouth.

Never in her life had she imagined being seduced by two men would be so incredible. Every nerve in her body simmered below boiling and juices coated the crotch of her bikini. Mitch's mouth continued to explore and tease hers while Jake softly bit at the side of her neck, sending shots of pleasure straight to her core. Mitch broke the kiss and moved to nibble at the other side of her neck. With a sigh, she sagged against Jake, letting his thick chest support her weakened body.

"Good girl, Tessa," Jake whispered. "But are you willing to take this a step further?"

"You mean both of you at once?" she asked. "A ménage?"

"Yes," Mitch answered in her ear, making her shiver. "But only if you're okay with it."

"Are the two of you okay with it?"

She was so turned on by the idea she could barely get the question out. Jake's hand feathered down her back and between her legs from behind. He tugged at the elastic of her swimsuit and slid his fingers along her wet slit. She wanted to collapse onto the sand and beg them to take her right here. Her pussy pulsed with the need to feel one or both of them fucking her senseless.

"We're okay with it, Tess," Mitch whispered. "We've each loved you separately. It's time we loved you together."

She bit at her lower lip and let her gaze wander down Mitch's tanned chest. Two scars were the only things marring his perfect flesh—one below his left pec, the other about midtorso, just above and to the right of his belly button. The other four were on his thighs, two on each. No wonder he'd been through so much rehab. He was probably there for months.

Leaning forward, she touched her lips to one of the scars and his muscles twitched on a sharp intake of breath.

A girl's squeal from farther down the beach made Tessa jerk upright and glance around quickly.

"We should probably take this inside," Mitch said as he stared at Jake over her shoulder.

"I agree," Jake answered and removed his hand from Tessa's pussy.

She moaned in response, then bit her lip, her face heating in embarrassment.

"Don't worry, Tessa," Jake whispered in her ear. "I can assure you, you'll get all you can handle."

Mitch wrapped her beach towel around her shoulders and helped her to stand. Her legs wobbled slightly and she leaned heavily on Jake, who continued to keep her hands pinned behind her. She liked being bound and at his mercy, but the image of being at both men's mercy really sent her heart fluttering.

It was a sexual fantasy come true. Each one of them was incredible in bed and each one had his own strengths when it came to satisfying women. Mitch had an incredible mouth. The man could make her come by just licking her nipples.

Jake was a great fuck. He loved to give orders and talk dirty. But his hard, forceful thrusts never failed to send her over the edge, shuddering in ecstasy.

On weak knees, she climbed the stairs of the back deck and stepped into the cool beach house. Before she even realized what happened, Jake lifted her and sat her on the table. His hips settled between her thighs and pressed his hard cock against her hot pussy. She gasped as his lips settled possessively over hers, and she raised her freed hands to wrap around his neck. With a groan, she returned his kiss with relish, her fingers fisting in his soft hair.

It was over far too soon. Jake broke the kiss and turned her head toward Mitch, who stood off to her side.

"My turn," Mitch murmured before slanting his lips across hers in an entirely different kiss, but no less possessive.

Jake's mouth moved to her breasts, his teeth nipping gently at her nipples. She whimpered into Mitch's kiss, completely overwhelmed with the feel of two mouths turning her to total mush. Breathing became increasingly difficult as Jake moved from one breast to the other, while Mitch nibbled along the side of her neck. His teeth scraped the sensitive flesh behind her ear and she shuddered from head to toe.

Laying her back onto the table, Jake hooked his fingers into her bikini bottoms and tugged, pulling them down her trembling legs. The wood of the table was cool against her back, which felt like it was on fire. Every part of her burned with quickening desire and lust and she dug her fingers into her hair, trying to keep herself from falling completely into a mindless mass.

"Mmm, you're wet, Tessa," Jake whispered as he slid his finger along her slit.

Her hips bucked as Mitch added his touch as well. His thick fingers gently circled the opening to her vagina, then lower, spreading her juices around the tight hole of her anus. With maddening slowness, Jake drew the flat of his tongue across her clit, making her groan loudly as hot sparks shot outward from her stomach.

This was crazy and wild and she loved every second of it. So much so, she wanted more.

"Guys, please," she pleaded, her breaths panting through the quiet room. "I need to come."

"Patience," Jake ordered. "You'll come when I tell you and not before."

She moaned and bit down on her lower lip, trying desperately to keep the orgasm at bay. As though reading each other's minds, the two of them separated her labia and slid their fingers deep at the same time. The walls of her pussy quivered around their fingers, pulling them deeper, begging for more.

Through heavy-lidded eyes, she watched as Mitch lowered his head and licked his tongue across her clit. She bucked wildly, desperate for the release that hung so close. His licks were soft, gentle, putting just enough pressure against her sensitive nub to make her want more. Juices poured from her body and slid between the globes of her ass, wetting the table beneath her.

Shaking her head, she groaned in desperation. "Oh God. I'm not sure I can stop it."

"You can and you will," Jake ordered.

"Jake." She panted. "Mitch, please."

Mitch removed his finger and changed positions, thrusting it into the tight hole of her ass. She gasped, lifting her hips higher off the table as they worked their fingers, pressing them together through the thin membrane that separated her two channels. Heat raced through her as she fought hard to keep herself under control. Jake loved doing this—seeing just how far he could push her before she lost it.

Each man leaned forward and suckled at her breasts. The two of them were so in tune with one another it was like having sex with just one man. Their touches were timed so perfectly; their mouths seemed to work as one mouth as they blazed a path up the sides of her neck with their lips.

"Please," she begged. "I need one of you to fuck me."

Both men stood and removed their swimming trunks. Jake sat in one of the chairs, pulling her onto his lap with her back against his chest.

"Take me inside you, Tessa," Jake whispered in her ear. "Take all of me."

Slowly, she settled her pussy against the head of his shaft, then pressed downward, taking every delectable inch into her body. Closing her eyes, she groaned as his thick girth stretched her aching channel, filling her to the womb. Mitch's lips covered hers in a wild kiss, his tongue fucking her mouth as Jake's cock fucked her pussy.

When he pulled away, she whimpered and watched in growing desire as he stood to his full height between her splayed thighs and settled his bulging cock before her mouth. Licking her lips, she grasped his thick shaft and ran her thumb around the tip, spreading the drop of precum that had escaped the purple head.

"Take me in your mouth, Tess," he rasped, the muscle in his jaw jerking violently.

She could tell by the strain on his face he held onto his control by a thin thread. His blue eyes were almost navy in his desire, and they closed on a ragged sigh as she licked her tongue across the tip of his cock. His taste was hot and salty, his length soft like velvet.

This was much easier than she imagined. As Jake filled her pussy from behind, over and over, her mouth sucked at Mitch's cock. Each pounding thrust from Jake made her suck Mitch harder, taking him deeper down her throat. The feeling was so heady, so wild and exciting, her whole body spasmed and shook with the need to feel her release.

Relaxing her throat, she swallowed Mitch and he gasped, his hips jerking forward. With her free hand, she cupped his balls, massaging and squeezing them.

"Damn, that feels good, Tess," he murmured.

His fingers buried in her hair, holding her steady as he gently thrust his cock in and out of her mouth. Jake matched his rhythm, then moved his fingers to toy with her clit. She groaned around Mitch's cock, her body convulsing wildly with the added pressure to the sensitive nub.

"You can come now, Tessa," Jake whispered. "Come for us, baby."

Letting go of her control, her body erupted into a ball of pleasure. Blinding light exploded behind her eyes and she sucked at Mitch harder, making him growl.

"Oh yeah, Tess."

With a jerk of his hips, he spilled his seed deep into her throat just as Jake thrust upward, spilling his seed into her still-spasming channel. Rocking her hips, she bucked wildly against Jake as the convulsions continued to race through her. Warm fluid rushed from her vagina as the spasms continued, until finally they subsided and she collapsed against Jake's chest in a spent heap.

Chapter Six

Mitch lay on the bed with Tessa snuggled between him and Jake. With a smile, he watched the setting afternoon sun cast shadows on her long, tanned legs. Her blonde hair spread out around her head and he softly brushed a stray lock from her eyes. Long lashes fluttered against her cheeks and he wondered what she was dreaming. Were they good dreams or was she having nightmares about their situation? He hoped they'd been able to make her forget for at least a while.

Sharing her with Jake had been much easier than he'd initially thought. At first the idea of Jake touching her had made his gut clench, but in reality it had seemed natural. Even though their styles of making love were different, when they shared a woman, they worked as one, their styles blending into something more in the middle.

It didn't surprise him that they'd both loved her beyond reason. What the hell would they do when all this was over? Could he walk away if she chose Jake? His heart nearly broke in half just thinking about it. Now that she was back in his life, he wasn't sure he could let her go again.

She stirred next to him and he glanced toward Jake to see if her movements had awakened him. His friend still lay motionless, his hand resting on Tessa's hip. Mitch softly skimmed his fingers along the flesh of her arm. She was so soft, so perfect. Goose bumps rose along her skin and he smiled. Even in her sleep, she responded to his touch.

With the tip of his finger, he circled her nipple. It hardened into a tiny bud and he flicked his thumb across the hard peak. She arched her back and her lips parted on a sigh, which made for a very sexy picture.

"Wake up, beautiful," Mitch whispered.

Her lids fluttered and she stared up at him, her lips spreading into a sleepy smile. "What time is it?"

"It's almost dinnertime," he answered, chuckling when her stomach growled in response.

Her face turned a light shade of pink. "I guess I'm hungry."

"You should be. You missed lunch."

"It's your fault," she grumbled, her nose crinkling in the most adorable frown.

"Mine?" Mitch asked in amusement. "I think it was Jake's fault myself."

"The hell it is," Jake growled from behind Tessa.

Mitch and Tessa laughed, and Jake rose up on his elbow to glare at them.

"Keep laughing, Mitch. See if I invite you for the party next time."

Instantly Mitch tensed, and Tessa rose up to a sitting position between the two of them. "Okay. Let's keep this civil. Please. I'm not strong enough to pull the two of you apart."

"It never comes to blows," Mitch said with a chuckle. "So don't worry. A few strong words, maybe a 'go to hell' every now and then, but never blows."

Jake rolled to his back and placed his hand behind his head. The smug smile on his face made Mitch grit his teeth, his playful mood quickly evaporating.

"There was that one time," Jake said.

"What time?" Mitch asked, confused. They'd never hit each other.

"When you were dog-ass drunk. It wasn't long after you were in rehab. You don't remember?"

"If I was dog-ass drunk, then most likely not."

"I tried to help you walk and you hit me, insisting you didn't need my help."

Mitch frowned, trying to remember what Jake was talking about, but for the life of him, he couldn't. With a shrug, he glanced at Tessa. "I don't have a clue."

Jake sighed and sat up. "Remember when you had the busted lip?"

"You said I fell," Mitch snapped.

Jake grinned. "You did. Right into my fist."

"You son of a bitch." Mitch ran a hand through his hair. "Why didn't you tell me you hit me?"

"I hit you to get you out of the bar. You were so drunk, it knocked you out."

"Why was he so drunk?" Tessa asked. Worry creased her brow, and Mitch could have kicked himself for even bringing this up.

"Mitch had a hard time when he first started rehab," Jake started to explain.

"About what?" Tessa asked.

"Jake," Mitch cautioned.

"It's over, Mitch. You proved them wrong. Get over it," Jake snarled toward Mitch, then turned back to Tessa. "When he was first shot, the doctors didn't think he'd walk again. Mitch had a hard time with that, as well as the rehab. It was taking much longer than Mitch wanted it to and he drowned his sorrows in whiskey. The alcohol made it that much harder for him to walk, and when I tried to help him, he snapped."

Tessa pinned Mitch with a sorrowful expression and he scowled. "Don't go there, Tess." The last thing he wanted was for her to feel pity for him.

"Don't go where? I'm just sorry I wasn't there for you. I had no idea what had happened."

Mitch sighed and leaned forward to place a soft kiss on her cheek. "Don't. I made it through and I proved them wrong. It about killed me doing it, but hey…" He smiled and chucked her under the cheek with his finger. "It was character building."

Tessa smiled slightly and Mitch's heart burst. God, he still loved her so much. How had he made it through all this time without her? He realized he knew how. He'd buried his feelings and tried to forget her. He'd almost done it, until the second he saw her standing in front of him.

"How about something to eat?" Jake asked as he stood.

Tessa's gaze wandered down his friend's form in interest, and a slight pang of jealousy gripped his chest. Shaking it off, Mitch refused to fall prey to that emotion. It would only cause problems. Jake loved her just as much as he did.

She started to leave the bed, but Mitch held her back with a hand on her wrist.

"Dinner sounds good," Mitch said, giving Jake a slight nod. "You get it started and we'll meet you down there in a few."

Jake studied him with narrowed eyes, then smiled slightly. "All right. I hope you like Chinese."

"I love Chinese." Tessa grinned and Jake nodded in acknowledgement before turning to leave the room.

"Is something wrong?" she asked, turning to look at Mitch.

"No. I just wanted to make sure you were okay."

"Why wouldn't I be?"

"The ménage thing. I know you've never done that before."

Her lips spread into a sensual smile and his cock hardened instantly. Damn.

"I can assure you I enjoyed it," she purred.

"Good," he said with a grin. "Because so did I."

His fingers reached out to brush across her nipples and her teeth bit down on her lower lip.

"But I also like being alone with you."

"Do you?" she whispered.

"Oh, yes." He crooked his finger, indicating she should come closer. "Come here, beautiful. Let's make use of the few minutes we have alone."

She leaned toward him with a smile and Mitch's heart skipped a beat as he waited for the touch of her lips on his. He loved the taste of her mouth, the feel of her silken tongue as it glided around his. Burying his hand in her hair, he tugged her closer, deepening the kiss. She tasted like lemons—minty lemons—and he sucked at her tongue for more of the sultry confection.

"Should we be doing this?" she murmured against his lips, and he gave her a light shove, pushing her to her back.

"You'll have time alone with me, as well as Jake." He settled on his elbow and splayed his hand over her belly button. Leaning down, he licked at her nipple, making her gasp. "But anytime you want both of us together, just say the word."

"Earlier was wild and definitely incredible," she whispered, her eyes closing on a sigh when his teeth nipped at the underside of her breast. "Mitch."

"You're such a delectable appetizer," he murmured, then chuckled at her soft giggle. "As much as I want to fuck the hell out of you, we should probably get downstairs and help Jake with dinner. If we don't, he'll pout all night."

Tessa giggled again. "Jake doesn't pout."

Mitch raised above her and smiled into her beautiful eyes. Her finger came up to trace his lips, her touch gentle and sweet. Turning his head slightly, he kissed her palm. "Move it, woman, before I change my mind."

* * *

Admiral Williams stared at his computer screen, scrolling through phone logs and bank accounts. Things were slowly starting to come together and he was shocked at what he was seeing. Damn son of a bitch. Just how high did this go? And what were they after?

He suspected the missiles. Any country would pay a fortune to get their hands on such advanced pieces of weaponry. Weaponry his daughter helped to design. But surely they wouldn't be dumb enough to steal one. It had to be something else. He had a terrible feeling in his gut he'd made a huge mistake handing her over to Sparks.

During the course of his investigations, he hadn't found anything on the men protecting her, but that didn't mean she wasn't in danger. He had to figure out where she was and add his own level of protection before the man in charge found out what he knew and went after her to get to him. If he hadn't already.

* * *

Jake sat at the table and watched Tessa pick at her food. She appeared distracted, worried.

"You need to eat more than that, Tessa. You missed lunch earlier," Jake said.

She raised her eyes and her brow crinkled into a confused frown. "I'm sorry. What did you say?"

"I said you need to eat, baby."

"I know." She sighed heavily and dropped her fork back onto her plate. The clang of flatware hitting china rang loudly in the quiet room. "I'm just not hungry."

"Hungry or not, Tess, you need to keep your strength up," Mitch argued.

"I know, I know," she said with a wave of her hand. "I've just got too much on my mind."

Jake reached across and covered her hand with his. Hers was cold and trembled slightly. "Whatever you decide, Tessa, will be fine. You make your decision without worrying about me or Mitch, understand?"

She gave him a tiny smile of thanks, and his heart fluttered like a teenager smitten with his first love. Actually she was his first love. His first and only. And it had turned into one hell of a mess with him and his best friend fighting for the same woman.

To his surprise, earlier that afternoon hadn't been as hard as he'd initially thought. Seeing her kiss Mitch and suck his cock had only fueled his own desire for her. The jealousy bug had remained dormant and his love for her had actually grown stronger. Even when he'd come down to cook dinner, knowing she and Mitch would probably have sex hadn't affected him any. At first the thought had nagged at him, but by the time he'd gotten downstairs, it had felt natural to let them have some time alone.

"Eat," he croaked, then cleared his throat, ignoring Mitch's amused expression. "I have a surprise for you for dessert."

"Really?"

Her eyebrow quirked adorably, and Jake swallowed his lust. God, the woman could be so sexy without even trying.

"Yes. Now be a good girl and do as you're told."

"Will you punish me if I don't?" she teased, and Mitch choked on his wine.

Jake pinned her with a level stare, trying to ignore the way her robe fell partially open, revealing a hint of her perky breasts. Her blonde hair fell about her shoulders in loose curls, and he fought back the urge to bury his hands in it and tug her face down to his crotch.

"Do as you're told and I'll reward you." He leaned forward and lowered his voice. "I think you'll like the reward much more than the punishment."

"I don't know, Jake. Your punishments can be an awful lot of fun."

"Hmmm," Mitch murmured. "Looks like you've met your match, Jake."

Jake turned to stare at his friend, whose eyes twinkled with a mixture of amusement and lust. "I think we both have."

Chapter Seven

Tessa grinned wickedly at the two of them. Mitch still wore a towel around his waist and Jake wore the swim shorts from earlier. Both men made such a gorgeous pair with their wide, muscular chests and trim stomachs. They looked good enough to eat and they could definitely take her mind off what was going on; that's exactly what she needed. She needed to forget for a while, to put her worry aside and just relax.

Lifting her fork, she took a bite of the ginger chicken and fried rice. The flavors blended in her mouth, and she closed her eyes with a sigh. Jake had always been able to cook. He was almost as good in the kitchen as he was the bedroom. Mitch, bless his heart, was good at grilled cheese. Unless he'd changed, which she didn't believe, considering it had been Jake who had cooked all the meals so far.

"Okay. I'm eating and anxiously awaiting this surprise you have for me," she purred toward Jake and grinned when the amber of his eyes glowed with passion.

"Eat every bite," Mitch said. "I have a feeling you're going to need it."

"So do I," she teased with a wink. "Do the two of you live together?"

Jake stared at her in surprise, then blinked. "Wow, quick change of subject," he said with a grin. "But yeah. Mitch and I share a condo. Have since he started at the agency."

"Sorry, but I have to take my mind off my surprise, otherwise I'll attack you right now."

Her pussy clenched at the heat she saw emanating from both their gazes. Wow, two men with the hots for her was most definitely a turn-on. Her palms began to sweat and she brushed her hand along the soft satin material of her robe. The action caused it to rub across her nipples and they hardened almost painfully. Glancing toward Mitch, she took another bite of food and used her other hand to gently pull the robe open a little more. His stare moved immediately to her cleavage, and she turned to catch Jake's stare there as well. She loved teasing them like this. She hadn't had this much fun in months.

With the tip of her toe, she kicked at Jake's leg, getting his attention. When his smoldering eyes met hers, she licked her lips seductively and moaned. "This Chinese is wonderful. Where did you learn to cook like this?"

He coughed and grabbed his glass to down a large sip of wine. "Didn't I ever tell you about that?" he asked.

"No. I don't think so," she purred and slowly slipped another bite into her mouth, her tongue flicking out to lick a stray piece of rice from her lip.

Jake growled softly and turned to his own plate.

"My mother was a chef and taught cooking lessons twice a week. I used to help her out. I think at first I did it to piss off my father. To him, cooking was for pansies." Jake shrugged and leaned back in his chair. "But cooking grew on me."

"You're certainly not a pansy, Jake," Tessa purred, then grinned. "And you're definitely a very good cook."

"Keeps me fat," Mitch said with a grin, making Tessa giggle.

"Undo your robe, Tessa," Jake ordered softly.

With a sultry smile, she untied her robe and separated it to expose her aching breasts. They both stared at her hungrily, and with a boldness she wouldn't have had earlier in her life, she brushed her fingers across her nipples to tease them.

"Now take it off, Tess. Let us see you eat in the nude."

She did as Mitch ordered and trailed her finger along her plate, scraping up a bit of ginger. Sticking her finger in her mouth, she licked it clean, smiling to herself when both men swallowed visibly. The ocean breeze blew through the open French doors and cooled her heated flesh, making her shiver slightly. It was amazing how fast they could make her hot.

"Your turn," she commanded as she licked the last of the spice from her knuckle.

Mitch lifted his hips and threw the towel to the floor. His cock sprang free, large and thick, the purple head engorged and leaking precum. Jake followed, his swimsuit joining Mitch's towel on the floor. His cock was slightly longer than Mitch's, but just as thick and the head just as engorged. They were perfect.

Licking her lips, she stared at the two of them, wondering which one she wanted first. Jake stood and moved to the kitchen counter, grabbing a pie. She sniffed with a smile as he set it before her on the table. Key lime. "Oh, God. I love key lime."

"I bet you've never had it like this before."

Grabbing her hands, Jake pulled them together behind the chair. She drew in a soft gasp of air, then slinked down slightly to get more comfortable. He used the belt from her robe, so the bindings weren't tight, but she knew not to undo them until told to.

"Are you going to feed me?" she asked over her shoulder. The very idea sent a tremor down her back and juices flowing from her pussy.

"In a manner of speaking," Mitch teased, then stuck his finger into the pie, covering it with cream and key lime filling before holding it before her lips.

She opened her mouth, allowing him to slide his finger inside, and she sucked every last drop of the dessert from his knuckles. His blue eyes narrowed in desire as her tongue circled the tip of his finger, making sure to get every last drop of the sweet pie.

Leaning down, Mitch's mouth covered hers and his tongue invaded, exploring her mouth and stealing the taste of the pie.

"Mmmm," Mitch murmured. "So sweet."

With his finger beneath her chin, Jake turned her so he could kiss her as well. He tasted of wine and ginger, and she moaned, her tongue trying to find more of his spicy taste.

"Oh yeah. Definitely sweet," he whispered, then stood, sticking his finger into the pie as well.

But instead of putting it into her mouth as she'd expect, he used his fingers to spread the confection between her legs. The cold cream at first made her gasp, but Jake's expert touch soon warmed her and made her squirm in her chair, desperate for more of the wicked sensation.

Mitch pulled her chair back, then kneeled between her legs. Warm fingers separated her labia before a warm tongue licked up her slit, causing her to almost buck from the chair. Jake straddled her hips, placing his key lime-covered cock in front of her mouth. She smiled, then leaned forward to lick across the tip of his shaft. He groaned, his hand gripping the base of his cock painfully hard. She'd never eaten key lime pie like this before.

With Mitch licking at her pussy the way he was, it was hard for her to concentrate on pleasing Jake. Her whole body burned with the need to come down Mitch's throat, to feel his tongue flicking at her clit. He did it so well, and she groaned, shifting her hips to give him better access.

Opening her eyes, she gazed up at Jake, trying to concentrate on his face and the strained look in his eyes. Slowly, she ran her tongue around his tip, then down the side, licking away all the cream. The sweet taste mixed with his salty one created a taste that was all Jake—one she knew she wouldn't be able to get enough of. With patience she never knew she had, she licked away every drop of cream before engulfing his cock within her mouth. The head of his shaft hit the back of her throat, and she relaxed, swallowing him farther.

Jake closed his eyes on a groan and pulled back slightly, before gently thrusting back in, filling her mouth and stretching her jaw. But she didn't care. She loved doing this to him. She loved his taste when he spilled his seed into her mouth.

He pulled away much too soon, and the two men switched places. Jake once again spread pie around her pussy, while Mitch covered his cock with the confection. She definitely liked eating dessert this way and anxiously waited for Mitch to slide his cock into her mouth. She lapped at his length, moaning as her lips licked away all the cream. Jake's mouth teased her clit, and his tongue slid into her sopping pussy, fucking her with it.

She gasped, her body so close to release it ached. "Jake…" she groaned around Mitch's cock, then growled when Jake pulled away just as she was about to burst. "No…" she protested.

"We're not done yet, Tessa," Jake admonished.

"You're killing me." She sighed and closed her eyes tightly. God, she wanted them. Both of them.

Jake moved behind her and released her bound hands. Holding his hand out, he waited for her to take it. Everything with Jake was about her accepting and following. He would never make her do something she didn't want to do, but at the same time, he always pushed her limits. Placing a petite hand in his, she followed him and Mitch to the couch, wondering what it was they had in mind.

"Lay on the couch, Tessa," Jake ordered, and she quickly made herself comfortable on the pillows.

Her heart raced wildly and her pussy clenched. If they didn't do something soon, she'd combust. She just knew it. Every nerve in her body screamed to be fucked and filled.

Mitch moved to quickly settle between her thighs on his knees. Putting his hands beneath her hips, he lifted her slightly and rubbed his length along her aching pussy. She groaned and moved with him, her legs lifting to settle over his shoulders.

Jake watched, his smoldering hot gaze devouring her. His hand gripped his cock and slowly worked up and down the long, thick length.

"Take him inside you, Tessa," Jake ordered. "I want to watch him fuck you."

Mitch slowly pushed his cock into her pussy. She closed her eyes and sighed as his cock filled her to the womb, stretching her, dominating her.

"Oh, yes," she growled as he plunged in and out, his balls slapping against her ass as he pushed deeper.

The couch sank as Jake settled over her, placing his knees on each side of her shoulders. He bent forward, his fingers gripping the armrest of the couch. His cock was right in front of her mouth, and she opened her lips in silent invitation. She wanted to taste him—to swallow his cum as Mitch fucked her.

Slowly, he pushed his cock farther into her mouth, but she wanted more and sucked harder, moving her lips up and down his length, matching Mitch's rhythm. Jake growled loudly and buried one hand in her hair, holding her head still. He took back control of the movements, keeping them slow and steady. Her jaw ached from being held open so wide, but she barely noticed. She wanted more of him and nipped at the purple head with her teeth.

"Oh, fuck," Jake groaned. "That felt good, baby."

“What the both of you are doing feels good,” she said with a sigh.

“Like this, Tess?” Mitch purred and flicked his thumb across her sensitive clit.

She screamed and bucked against him. “Oh, yes. Oh, God. I like it.”

Opening her lips, she sucked again at Jake’s cock. Harder and faster she worked her mouth, determined for him to come before she did. Jake let go of her hair, allowing her the control, and she let herself go, sucking every last inch of him down her throat.

Her body tensed as Mitch continued to play with her clit, his cock seeming to swell even larger as he kept pounding at her pulsing body. Her legs shook and her stomach spasmed as the first waves of her climax swept through her. Moaning around Jake’s cock, she raised a hand and began to massage his balls. His moan let her know he liked what she did. Giving him a final squeeze, she slid her finger along the cleft of his ass and circled the tight hole of his anus.

He groaned in warning, but Tessa ignored him, sliding her finger knuckle deep into his tight passage. He gasped and jerked his hips forward. She kept fucking his ass with her finger, finding that tiny spot inside him that would send him reeling. Mitch’s thrusts increased, pounding against her harder, his cock forging deeper as her body erupted into shattering bliss. Tingling spasms raced through her limbs and she sucked at Jake harder, her body riding the wave of ecstasy.

Mitch tensed and shouted just as Jake growled and spilled his seed deep into her throat. It was warm and salty, and she licked away every last drop he spewed forth as though she were starving. She kept grinding her hips against Mitch and sucking at Jake until every last pulse had been spent and her body relaxed.

"Where the hell did you learn that?" Jake asked as he moved from her shoulders and dropped to his knees on the floor by her head.

"I read a lot," she said with a sigh.

* * *

Scott continued his search through the admiral's log cabin, finding nothing. He stopped, his head tilting to the side to listen. Footsteps came from the living room area. Reaching behind him, he pulled his gun from the holster at the small of his back. The security system had been turned off and trashed. No evidence would be found there, but it also left them in the dark as to who else might be in the massive house.

On pins and needles, he waited. The swinging door opened and Scott raised his gun, ready to shoot the intruder, then sighed as soon as he recognized the man standing before him.

"Damn, it's you," Scott said with a growl and lowered the gun.

"Nice to see you too," he snarled. "What did you find?"

"Nothing."

"Nothing at all?" the man asked.

"Do I need to write it out for you in crayon?" Scott asked with a disgusted wave of his hand. "I said nothing."

"The boss wants Admiral Williams found now."

"It's time to use the girl, then."

Scott nodded and flipped his phone open to make the call. They'd use Tessa to lure the admiral out of hiding. One way or another, they'd get what they were after.

Chapter Eight

Feeling a little better, Tessa pulled brownies from the oven and began to cut them into small squares. They were still really hot, but she knew Mitch liked them that way. With a smile, she remembered how he would sometimes eat them straight from the pan. She often wondered how he could eat the way he did and still look so good.

Placing several pieces on a plate, she headed to the living room where Jake and Mitch sat watching the news. The sun had set, and instead of lights, they'd lit candles, making the room smell like lavender mixed with the salty smell of the ocean. A bottle of wine sat on the coffee table along with three glasses. What were the two of them up to?

"What's this?" she asked, nodding toward the bottle of wine.

"Something to help you relax," Jake said as he stood and took the plate of brownies from her hand.

Mitch turned off the television and moved to the couch, patting the spot next to him indicating she should sit.

Jake smiled and leaned forward to place a bite of brownie on her tongue. "You know, the three of us together has kind of grown on me."

"It has me, too," Mitch said with a snort of surprise. "We need to figure out what to do about it."

"Yeah, but not now," Jake murmured as he placed another bite of brownie on Tessa's tongue. "I'm having too much fun at the moment."

The warm chocolate filled her mouth just as the love shining from Jake's eyes filled her heart. Glancing at Mitch, she noticed the same love sparkling in his gaze as well, and her chest swelled with pride and love of her own. Never could she imagine two men like this both loving her, giving her everything she could possibly want. But could it really work, or were they all living in a fantasyland?

Mitch poured wine into her glass and she slowly sipped at the spicy beverage. Her limbs began to tingle and her body heated. Whether from the wine or the sultry stares, she wasn't sure.

"The two of you are going to spoil me," she said with a giggle.

"That's the general idea," Mitch purred suggestively. "We want you so happy and content you'll never want to leave."

Tessa smiled and ran her finger down Mitch's hard chest. The muscles twitched beneath her finger as she moved lower and slowly circled an erect, brown nipple.

"You're both so gorgeous," she whispered. The wine was starting to make her feel just a little light-headed. So sleepy. "How did you get to be so big?"

"We came out that way," Jake said with a grin.

"I don't think our cocks are what she was talking about," Mitch answered in amusement. "Nor do I think our little Tess holds her liquor well."

With a nod of his head, he indicated how hard a time she was having keeping her eyes open. Why was she so tired? Closing her eyes, she rested her head against Jake's shoulder. The slow, rhythmic beating of his heart lulled her into a deep sleep.

Jake brushed her hair aside with a slight smile. She looked so frail and innocent lying between them like this. "My guess, it's stress. She's had a rough couple of days."

"Why don't you take her upstairs and put her in bed," Mitch offered as he set the half-eaten plate of brownies on the coffee table. "We need to talk anyway."

Jake nodded his head in agreement and shifted to circle her shoulders with one arm then slide the other under her thighs. She weighed practically nothing and he lifted her easily. Her head settled back against his shoulder as she snuggled closer to his chest, perfectly curled against him. Taking the steps slowly, he headed to her bedroom and laid her in the king-sized bed. He and Mitch would join her later, but Mitch was right. They needed to talk about this situation with Tessa.

And the sooner the better.

* * *

Tessa awoke with a start and stared at the open bedroom door. She wasn't sure what the noise was that had awakened her or why it had frightened her so much. Had she been having a bad dream? Raising her hand, she brushed a stray hair from her eyes. She didn't think so, but she couldn't remember.

A loud bang sounded from downstairs followed by a grunt of pain. What the hell was that? "Jake?" she whispered loudly. Another loud noise followed by glass breaking. "Mitch!" she screamed.

Her heart pounded hard in her chest as she jumped from the bed and grabbed the small pistol she'd hidden in her laptop case. She was surprised neither of the men had found it and asked her about it. Checking the chamber, she flipped off the safety and crept from the room.

As carefully as possible, she leaned over the railing to see the bottom floor. Another bang, followed by what sounded like a wooden table splintering. What was going on down there, and why weren't they answering her?

Taking the steps one at a time, she slowly began to move. Halfway down, a man was thrown across the room and landed with a thud at the bottom of the staircase. He was dressed in black, a ski mask over his face. She gasped, her hands beginning to tremble in real fear. Had they found them?

Jake came into view at the far end of the living room. He leaned over another body lying on the floor. She could see his lips moving and knew he must be talking with Mitch, but couldn't hear what he was saying. A movement at the bottom of the stairs caught her eye and she watched in terror as the man slowly reached for something in his boot. He picked his shoulders partially off the floor and drew his hand back as though to throw what looked like a knife. Raising her gun, she took aim, and without thinking, fired.

The man fell back to the floor with a cry, then silence. She couldn't move. Her hands trembled as she stared at the man she'd killed. She'd actually killed a man, and for a split second, she felt ill. Like she might throw up the brownies and wine she'd had earlier. Swallowing her bile, she tried to lower the gun but couldn't. She couldn't move.

"Tessa," Jake whispered.

She could hear him, feel his presence next to her, but she couldn't answer him.

"Tessa, baby. Let me have the gun."

Slowly his hand covered hers. His warmth seeped into her flesh, and she began to tremble in earnest, but couldn't release her grip.

"Tessa. Give me the gun," he said, this time a little more firm.

Mitch came up the stairs behind Jake, his gaze full of concern. Her grip released and she felt the gun being pulled from her grip. Mitch squeezed past Jake and cupped her face, forcing her to look at him. "Look at me, Tess. Not the body. Look at me."

Her gaze turned to Mitch, and she didn't miss the worry and fear she saw etched in his face. "Are you okay?" he asked.

"I…I…um…"

"Deep breaths, Tess. Take a deep breath," Mitch instructed, and she did as he said, pulling air deep into her lungs and letting it out slowly.

"Where the hell did you learn to shoot?" he asked.

"Daddy," she answered.

"Shooting people is a lot different from shooting targets, huh?" Mitch teased, trying to make her relax.

She shook her head, her lower lip trembling with oncoming tears.

"Don't cry, baby," Jake said from behind her and placed an arm around her shoulders, hugging her against his chest. "You did good. You saved our necks. We know better."

Sirens blared as police cars quickly surrounded the small house. Flashing lights bathed the room in blue and red, and Tessa stiffened, her frightened gaze darting toward the growing number of cars outside. "Oh, God." She sighed. "Who called them?"

"My guess is the neighbors," Jake said with a sigh. "We weren't exactly quiet."

"I'll take care of it," Mitch said and moved quickly to the door, holding his hands toward the ceiling in surrender. In his right one, his NCIS badge. "NCIS agent," he shouted toward the surrounding officers. "I need to speak to the man in charge."

Tessa watched as two men came forward, one keeping his gun on Mitch the entire time, the other studying his badge. Once he was satisfied, Mitch took him to the side and explained the situation.

"How did they find us?" Tessa asked.

"Who packed your suitcases?" Jake asked.

"My assistant. Why?"

"Come with me."

Taking her hand, Jake pulled her up the stairs. In her room, he grabbed her bags and threw them on the bed, dumping all the contents into huge piles. "Jake," she argued. "What are you doing?"

"Looking for something," he said as he tugged at the seams, separating the fabric. It gave way with a loud tear, and Jake stuck his hand inside, ripping it even more as he went.

"Looking for what?"

He pulled his hand out and held up a small round object with a thin wire hanging from the center. "This," he said.

"Is that what I think it is?"

"GPS tracking transmitter. How well do you know your assistant, Tessa?"

"No." She shook her head firmly. Kate was her friend.

"How long have you known her?"

"Six months. She wouldn't do this, Jake. She's my friend."

"Hell of a friend," Jake snarled.

With determined strides, he headed to the adjoining bathroom and dropped the transmitter into the toilet, flushing it down the drain. Mitch stuck his head in the door, startling Tessa. She jumped and spun around, a shaking hand coming to rest on her chest.

"You all right?" Mitch asked.

He stepped close to her and grasped her shoulders in a comforting grip. His blue eyes studied her, and she smiled slightly, trying to put him at ease. "I'm okay. You just startled me."

"I'm sorry, Tess." His fingers brushed lightly across her cheek, burning a path straight to her stomach.

"How did it go with the police?" Jake asked from the bathroom door.

"Fine. It's all straightened out. He's just pissed no one told him we were here."

"Like we're supposed to," Jake snarled. "Isn't that the whole idea of a safe house?"

Mitch's gaze strayed to the bed and the pile of clothes scattered about. "Something you want to tell me?" he asked, his eyebrow raised in question.

"Jake found a GPS transmitter."

Mitch's expression suddenly turned to one of worry. "Where?"

"In the lining of her suitcase," Jake answered. "I'm sure there're more, though."

"Ditch it. We'll get new stuff where we're going."

"What?" Tessa gaped. "What about my clothes?"

"They're compromised, Tess," Mitch said. "Pick out one outfit and let Jake go over it really well to make sure there's nothing hidden in the seams. The rest of it stays here."

"Even my purse?"

"Yep," Mitch said, then turned to leave the room. "I'll get our stuff together. Tess, you get to work on yours. We need to hurry. The sooner we get out of here, the better."

Tessa growled in aggravation. How could she leave all her stuff behind? Her wallet, her credit cards, her checkbook? It was crazy.

"You can take the personal stuff out of the wallet, Tessa," Jake said from behind her. "But the wallet itself has to stay behind."

She threw her hands out, then dropped them back down. Her palms landed against her thighs with a slap. Looked like she didn't have much of a choice. "All right," she sighed.

As quickly as possible, she found a lightweight capri set, then frowned. "Mitch?" she called out.

"Yeah?" he answered back, his deep voice carrying down the hall.

"Where are we going? Do I need warm clothes or something cool?"

"Warm clothes."

She caught Jake's stare as he leaned against the bathroom doorjamb and pursed her lips. "Warm clothes. Real informative, isn't he?"

Jake chuckled. "I'm sure we'll find out soon enough. How about the jeans and sweater? That will be easy to check and will look good on you too."

He leered as his gaze wandered down her form in a slow process that made her flesh burn. His eyes seemed to glow like heated embers, and her nipples hardened beneath the thin material of her robe. It didn't escape his notice. He sauntered over and brushed his thumb across one of her hard nipples with a grin. A tremble skimmed along her limbs as they stared at one another, the desire they felt shining in their hot gazes.

"Hurry up, guys. We have to go."

Mitch's shouted words from across the hall startled her back to the present, and she quickly grabbed an outfit, then handed it to Jake to go over. He was right. They needed to get out of here before someone else showed up.

Chapter Nine

Tessa slouched onto the leather chair with a sigh. Mitch and Jake's soft voices carried through the cabin from the cockpit, but she didn't really listen. Stress and fatigue weighed heavily on her shoulders. She turned to stare out the window, but even the fluffy white layers of soft clouds below them couldn't take her mind off what had happened the night before.

They'd left the airport about thirty minutes ago, but she still had no idea where they were headed. They hadn't told her and she hadn't asked. The clouds obscured the view of the landscape below, so even that didn't offer up any clue. Finally, tired of being left out of the loop, she leaned over the side of her chair and glanced back toward the cockpit.

"Hey, guys. Want to tell me where we're headed?"

Jake stood in the doorway, his hips leaning against the jamb. One hand rested in the pocket of his navy blue Dockers, while the other rested against the opposite jamb. He stopped talking to Mitch and turned to smile down at her.

"Getting anxious?" he asked.

"No. Bored and tired of being in the dark. Where are we going?"

"Someone's in a mood," Mitch teased.

"Be nice," Jake joked at Mitch, then shut the cockpit door and came to sit on the sofa across from Tessa. "We're headed to Tennessee. Mitch called and reserved us a secluded cabin in the Smoky Mountains above Gatlinburg. We should be safe there."

"We hope." Tessa sighed and fingered the two photos of Mitch and Jake she had in her hand. She couldn't leave those behind, and she'd been holding them since they'd left.

"Come here, Tessa." Jake patted the seat of the sofa next to him.

Standing, she moved to sit close to Jake, letting his warm body relax her tense one. His arm circled her shoulders, pulling her close, and she rested her head on his shoulder. His heart beat a steady rhythm beneath her ear, and she inhaled deeply the smell of musk and man. Jake didn't need cologne. He had his own special smell.

"We're going to be fine," Jake said as he kissed the top of her head.

Reaching out, he took the small photos of him and Mitch from her fingers. The heat of a blush moved up her cheeks and she licked her lips. "I had those in my wallet."

Jake smiled and pulled his own wallet from his pants. Opening it, he dug into a small compartment and pulled out a photo. He handed it to her, the corner of his mouth tilting in a slight grin. She took it and stared at the picture of her and Jake with a surprised smile. It had been taken the weekend they'd spent at the beach. They'd gone to a new nightclub and spent the evening dancing. Someone at the club had taken the picture.

"I remember this," she said. "I can't believe you still have it."

He shrugged and slipped the picture back into its hiding place. "I wanted something to remember you by."

"Same with me. Kate caught me staring at them the day Sparks took me into protective custody. I'm still having a hard time with Kate being in on all this. She was my friend. Or at least I thought she was. I always felt I could talk to her. Tell her anything."

Jake squeezed her shoulders, but remained silent. His fingers began a slow, tantalizing trail down to her elbow, then back up again.

"If it was her that put the trackers in my luggage, how do you suppose she got involved?" she asked quietly, trying to ignore what his touch was doing to her insides.

Turning, she rested her cheek and one of her hands against his chest. His heart beat a slow rhythm under her ear. It made her feel safe and secure, and she snuggled closer to his warmth.

"She could have been involved from the start. We may never know for sure. Mitch called the director and told him. Sparks is going to put a tail on her and see where she goes. If it was her, maybe she'll lead us to the inside man."

"I don't believe it is, Jake. I refuse to accept that she would be involved in something like that, that she would try to hurt me."

"I know." Jake sighed, his chest lifting, then sinking back. "I hope, for your sake, it's not her."

Despite the topic of conversation, she couldn't sit this close to him and not touch him. Her finger slipped past the buttons of his red shirt and toyed with the smooth skin of his chest. She could feel the heat emanating from him. It was like being next to a small smoldering fire—so warm and comforting. Her thumb flicked at the button, freeing it from the hole so she could slide her whole palm along his flesh.

Jake remained quiet, allowing her to explore at her leisure. In her ear, his heart rate increased and his breathing quickened as she moved her hand to circle his taut nipple. The muscles bunched and twitched beneath her touch as she released more buttons and moved lower along the hard ridges of his abdomen.

"You work out a lot," she stated softly, her fingers working beneath the waistband of his pants.

"Depends on what you call a lot," he murmured.

His hand moved to undo the button and zipper of his slacks so her hand would fit inside. Slowly, she worked lower, rubbing across the hard ridge beneath his boxer shorts. She gently squeezed him and he moaned, his fingers digging into the flesh of her shoulder.

"I would have to say, with this physique"—she said softly, her voice tantalizing, her nails softly scratching at the head of his shaft through the thin cotton—"that it's at least four days a week. Am I close?"

"Close," he growled into her ear. "You're also very close to getting fucked. And good."

"Here in this plane?" she teased. "Aren't you the bad boy?"

Jake chuckled and grabbed her hand, slipping it under the elastic band of his shorts. "Baby, you have no idea."

His cock was hot and velvety, thick and long. Just thinking about him sliding that glorious piece of flesh into her pussy made her breath catch. It jerked beneath her touch as she slowly worked her hand up and down, her own body growing more desperate to take him inside it.

Removing her hand, she turned to straddle his lap, her legs on either side of his hips. Her aching pussy settled against his shaft, and she moaned, pressing down harder. Even through their clothes, she could feel his steely length. His power. His hands gripped her hips, moving her against him in a maddeningly slow rhythm.

"Take off your sweater, Tessa," Jake ordered, the strain in his voice evident.

Grabbing the hem, she taunted him by slowly pulling it up and over her head. She dropped it to the floor, watching as Jake's eyes began to glow with a hunger that threatened to burn her across the scant inches that separated them. She flicked her tongue out, running it across her dry lips. Jake growled and squeezed her breasts together, then tugged at the lace of her bra, freeing them. He covered her nipples with his mouth and sucked with an animalistic growl deep in his chest, and she gasped in surprise and increasingly burning lust. Burying her fingers in his hair, she arched her back, freely giving more.

His mouth was hot and his tongue wicked as it flicked across her sensitive peaks. Wetness poured from her pussy, coating the crotch of her panties.

"Jake," she cried, then gasped as he pressed upward against her aching mound.

Rubbing against him like she was had her so close she could taste it. Her release skimmed just under the surface, and she wanted him inside her desperately. Her hips began to undulate faster, harder, increasing the friction along her slit. She was so close, so turned on.

With his hands at her waist, he picked her up and tossed her to her back on the couch. She giggled and lifted her hips so he could slide her jeans off and throw them to the floor. His mouth covered her hot mound through the lace of her underwear, and she bucked her hips upward, fighting off the first throbs of her release. God, the man was driving her crazy with lust. She loved it when he was this way. So out of control and wild—passionate. Hooking his fingers into the elastic, he tugged her panties down and they joined the jeans on the floor.

His eyes seared her flesh as he stood and removed his pants as well. His cock sprang free, hard and long and thick. She licked her lips, anxious for the feel of his shaft driving into her, hard and deep. How had it gone from comforting to fucking in just a matter of minutes? How was it he could make her forget her troubles and where they were?

Settling on his knees between her thighs, he lifted one of her legs and settled it over his shoulder. The other he left lying on the couch. Never taking his eyes from hers, he placed his palms on the cushions by her head and used the tip of his cock to toy with her pussy, spreading the juices along her slit. She sighed and closed her eyes in pleasure, enjoying the feel of his length sliding through her cream.

"No," Jake commanded. "Look at me. I want to see your eyes when I fuck you."

The second she opened her gaze and locked it with his, he thrust deep, practically taking the very air from her lungs. She shouted and lifted her hands to grip the arm of the couch behind her head. Her nails dug into the soft leather fabric as he pounded into her over and over, filling her so completely she couldn't catch her breath.

Harder, he thrust into her, his balls slapping at her ass as he pushed even deeper. Her breasts, still held captive by her lowered bra, jiggled with every pounding movement of his hips. His jaw clenched and his eyes glazed over as they stared at one another, neither willing to let the other go from their sight. She wanted to come, needed to. Every nerve in her body tingled, and her stomach tensed as the need became stronger, more urgent.

She knew Jake and knew he would tell her when she could let go. They would come together. They always did. She loved how he spilled his seed deep within her pussy just as her body erupted. Would he come with her or would he make her hold off?

"Jake," she sighed. "I need to come. Come with me."

He growled in answer and ground his hips against her swollen clit, making her groan in sheer delight. It was exactly what she needed, and her body exploded. Her pussy spasmed around his cock, pulling him deeper, sucking at his cock. With a shout, he erupted inside her, his cock twitching and throbbing, creating another small wave of pleasure that skimmed along her passage.

He sighed and released her leg from his shoulder. His warm body settled over hers, pushing her into the now-heated leather at her back.

"I love you, Tessa," he whispered.

She closed her eyes, holding on to those four words that meant so much to her, but at the same time broke her heart. What if she didn't choose Jake?

* * *

When they arrived at the airport in Sevierville, Tennessee, the local flight base of operations had a rental car waiting for them. One credit card, three pages of paperwork, and thirty minutes later, they were on their way to the tourist town of Pigeon Forge. The car rental agent had told them that was a good place to go shopping.

Tessa was relieved, for she was in dire need of clothes. She was also relieved they hadn't really planned to keep her naked the whole time, which Mitch had teased her about once they'd landed. It was a beautiful day, though chilly, and she wrapped her arms around herself in an effort to keep warm, while Mitch gave instructions for them to have the Lear gassed up and ready so they could leave without too many hassles.

Once in the car, a silver Grand Am, Mitch turned on the heat so she could get warm. She smiled in thanks, then glanced away guiltily, her gaze straying to the beautiful mountain scenery. Every time she looked at Mitch she felt terrible. She tried to tell herself that Mitch had told her earlier she would have time with each of them alone, but still it felt odd and way too much like she'd cheated on him.

Reaching across the front seat, Mitch gave her knee a squeeze to get her attention. When she looked over at him, he silently mouthed the words "It's okay," then smiled sweetly.

She frowned, making him chuckle. Did he know what she and Jake had done?

"I know," he whispered softly. "I heard. Don't feel guilty."

Opening her mouth, she gaped at him. He'd heard them? "This doesn't bother you?" she asked, then glanced over her shoulder to see Jake still focused on the open laptop on his knees.

He inclined his head to the side with a slight shrug. "It did at first, but now…I don't know. It just seems normal."

"The two of you are just too weird." She sighed.

Mitch laughed and patted her knee. "No. We're just two halves of the same whole. We both love you, Tess. We both will always love you."

Her small hand covered his, and he twisted his fingers, entwining them with hers. Would she ever feel as comfortable with this situation as they did? In the end, could she hurt one or both of them? How was she going to make this choice?

Traffic began to slow as congestion built along the four-lane highway leading into the mountain town of Pigeon Forge. It was very similar to Branson, Missouri, with all the dinner theaters with live country music shows, and of course, Dollywood. The cold weather didn't seem to affect tourism. The town was packed, and it took them over an hour to make the twelve-mile drive from Sevierville.

Toward the middle of town and on their left was a huge outlet mall with all kinds of shops. Mitch pulled into the parking lot and found a parking spot toward the far end.

"We're here," Mitch said with a grin toward Tessa. "Ready for some shopping?"

"I'm always ready for shopping," Tessa answered. "But I thought we were staying in Gatlinburg?"

"We are. Gatlinburg is another six miles that way." Mitch raised his hand and pointed toward the mountains ahead of them. "We'll head there and get checked into our cabin after we get you some clothes."

"We should also stop at a grocery store," Jake chimed in, saying the first thing since they'd left the airport.

"You want to take the car and do that while Tessa and I shop? It'll save time."

Jake nodded and closed down his computer. The three of them climbed from the car, and Jake made his way to the front seat. A cold mountain wind whipped through her thin sweater, making her shiver in surprise. The car had been so warm, the sudden gust of cold air was a shock to her body.

Before settling in, Jake grabbed Tessa's arm and tugged her to him. His warm lips slanted across her chilled ones, and she sighed, opening her lips so he could slip his tongue inside and gently plunder before breaking the all-too-short kiss.

"Buy something sexy," he murmured with a grin, then climbed into the driver's seat. "I'll call you when I'm done to find out where you are," Jake said with a nod toward Mitch, who nodded in acknowledgement.

They silently watched him back out and waved as he pulled away toward the store they'd passed just down the road. Taking her hand, Mitch gave it a gentle squeeze and placed a soft kiss against the side of her neck. "Alone at last," he teased. "Want to find an empty bathroom stall?"

Tessa giggled. "You wouldn't."

"Have sex with you in a public bathroom? Hell yeah, I would."

Laughing harder, Tessa shoved at his hard chest, pushing him toward the mall. "Clothes, remember. You can fuck me later."

Mitch wiggled his eyebrows playfully as he tugged on her hand, pulling her along after him. "How is it you know so much about this place? You seem to know your way around pretty well."

"Jake and I grew up not far from here. We spent a lot of summers here and in Gatlinburg. We especially enjoyed the rod runs."

"Rod runs?" she asked, intrigued.

"Yeah. It's where people bring their old, fixed-up cars and show them off. They have them about twice a year and it's always packed. Jake and I would bring his dad's restored Mustang. The girls loved it."

Tessa cringed, a sudden wave of jealousy forging a knot in her stomach. The thought of Jake and Mitch with other women didn't sit well with her, even if it was over ten years ago. "I'm sure the hussies did," she grumbled, making Mitch chuckle.

"Are you jealous?" he asked, holding the door open so she could step inside the warm mall.

"Of course not," she replied, then brushed past him, ignoring his chuckle. Pursing her lips, she eyed him from the corner of her eye. "Okay, maybe a little. And yes, I know it was over ten years ago, but still..." She shrugged.

"I know exactly how you feel," Mitch said with a smile. "I don't like the idea of other men touching you either. Past or present. Unless it's Jake," Mitch added with a frown.

"Have you and Jake shared a lot of women?" she asked hesitantly as they made their way down the wide hallway.

"You're just a glutton for punishment, aren't you?" Mitch teased.

"Just curious," she said with a shrug. "The two of you seem to work so well together."

Mitch chuckled. "I refuse to answer that question on the grounds that it may incriminate me."

"Chicken," she taunted.

His lips lifted in a sideways grin as he made a noise like a chicken, making Tessa laugh.

"So you and Jake grew up here," she said, changing the subject as they stepped into a shop. Her hands ran over beautiful sweaters in shades of fall colors.

"Yeah. My grandparents raised me until they died my senior year in high school. My grandfather had a friend in Congress who paved the way for me to go to the Naval Academy after graduation. If it hadn't been for him, I'm not sure what I would have done with my life. After graduating the Academy, I decided to try being a SEAL."

"Is it as tough as they say?" she asked. "My father was one years ago, but he never talked about it."

"You try to forget everything about the training except what you need. Imagine hell, then imagine it three times as bad. That will give you SEAL training."

She cringed and pulled a sweater off the shelf to get a closer look. "Why would you do that?"

"For the glory," he said with a grin. "And the women. They love a bad-ass SEAL.

Tessa snorted. "You're teasing."

He smiled. "I think that, honestly, at the time, I was on a mission to prove something. Either that or I secretly had a death wish. Have I not ever told you this?"

She shook her head. "No. When we dated before, we really didn't talk about things like this much. You avoided talk of your work."

"I did?" he asked with a frown, and Tessa turned to stare at him.

"Yes. You did," she said with a grin. "Stop acting like you don't remember what you were like. You were very tight-lipped."

"I know," he relented. "I was too tight-lipped. Especially when it came to you."

She smiled and kissed his cheek. "You know what? It's in the past. We're here now, so let's make the best of it."

He reached out and tugged at a small curl. "Deal."

The next hour or so went great. They moved from shop to shop, trying on clothes and joking about bad outfits. All through the mall she caught women admiring Mitch's body in his tight jeans and blue Atlanta Braves T-shirt. She couldn't blame them. He looked good enough to eat. Especially that ass. Levi's never looked so good.

"Stop staring at my ass, Tess, or we'll be finding that bathroom."

Tessa glanced up immediately, realizing he'd caught her admiring his attributes. She grinned wickedly, determined for a little payback. "I was just wondering what a butt plug would look like stuck up that ass."

Mitch raised an eyebrow, then snorted. "That's an image, I can assure you, you'll just have to continue to wonder about." He stepped closer and whispered suggestively in her ear. "Although, I bet a butt plug in your ass would be an incredible turn-on."

"What if I said I had one in there now?"

"I'd say you were lying, but the image is certainly worth thinking about." His lips softly touched her neck, and a shiver skimmed all the way to the base of her spine. "Let's get back to shopping before I decide to seriously consider the bathroom idea."

Tessa giggled, then glanced around at the people watching them. Her face heated in embarrassment before following Mitch into the nearest dress shop. Twelve outfits, three pairs of shoes, and numerous underclothes later, Jake called to say he was in the parking lot. Loaded with packages, they made their way to the entrance Jake indicated and met him outside. Jake made room for all her packages in the backseat, since the trunk was full of groceries.

"Just how long are we staying?" she asked upon seeing the multitude of filled bags.

"As long as necessary," Jake said with a smile. "But you can bet I'm in no hurry."

"Me either," Mitch said with a pat on her behind to move her along.

Tessa couldn't help but smile at the two of them. Every second, it seemed, she fell a little more in love. At the moment, she was so turned on it was pathetic. For the last two and a half hours, all she could think about was Mitch and the possibilities of a butt plug. She wished she had one. Just as she thought it, Jake slipped a bag into her hand. Curious, she glanced inside at all the sexual toys, including a butt plug, then laughed.

"Oh my God." Turning to Jake, she gaped at him. "Where on earth did you get all this?"

He shrugged. "A store I found. While you were trying on clothes, Mitch called and told me about your conversation."

Spinning around, she stared at Mitch in shock. "You told him about our conversation?"

Mitch smiled that sexy smile of his that always turned her knees to mush. "The image was just too tempting to pass up."

"The two of you are unbelievable."

Jake laughed and placed a kiss on her cheek. "Just relax and enjoy the ride, Tessa," he purred.

Chapter Ten

Stepping out onto the deck of the log cabin, Tessa admired the view of Gatlinburg below them. The sun had begun to set and the town's lights twinkled in the golden glow of twilight. She couldn't wait until tomorrow, so they could go exploring. She'd never been here and wanted to see as much as she could.

Jake had been a little leery about the idea, but Mitch seemed to think it would be okay if they were careful. So the decision had been made. They'd head out right after breakfast.

The cabin had been another surprise. She was expecting something primitive, but instead, it was quite the opposite. It had two bedrooms, both with king-sized beds. A massive fireplace stood in the center of the room with a loft overhead sporting a pool table, ping-pong table, and an air hockey table. The kitchen was every cook's wet dream, and the living room had leather furniture and a big-screen TV. Even the deck was high-tech, with an outdoor kitchen and massive hot tub overlooking the incredible view.

After arriving, she'd taken a shower in the huge tile shower, then put on the silk robe Mitch had picked out. Underneath she was nude and hot. Her nipples tingled as they rubbed along the satin fabric. All through her shower, she'd thought about her men. They were below, unloading the car, but more than anything she wanted them in the shower with her, touching her, licking at her pussy with their tongues, filling her with their cocks. She'd really worked herself into a frenzy, and when Jake came up behind her, placing his hand on her shoulder, she gasped, both in shock and desire.

"Be still," Jake commanded in his usual tone, and every nerve ending in her body sparked to life.

His hand gently lifted the hem of her robe and slid up along the outside of her thigh. Her muscles tensed in anticipation of his touch between her legs, but instead, he gently massaged the globes of her ass. With a tender touch, he slid something cold and wet down the cleft of her ass. Instantly, she realized it was one of the butt plugs, and her heart began to race wildly in her chest.

Slowly, he inserted it and her eyes closed on a sigh. Her tongue flicked out to lick her dry lips as he gently slid it in and out, teasing her beyond reason. Her pussy clenched, and juices poured from her body to wet the inside of her thighs. Jake's hot breath brushed along her neck, and she shivered as molten lust ran through her veins.

Pushing the plug as deep as it would go, he sucked at the side of her throat and pressed his hard cock into her hip, sending little shots of pleasure to her core. "Just a little taste of what's to come," he whispered.

"Can't it come now?" She sighed, wiggling her hips against his growing erection. "I've been thinking about this all day."

"Mitch is in the kitchen. Go talk him into it."

She smiled, knowing that wouldn't be hard at all. Jake gave her a gentle shove, and she walked slowly into the kitchen where Mitch stood chopping vegetables for dinner. In her mind, dinner could wait. She wanted them fucking her senseless now.

Coming to a stop on the other side of the kitchen island, she opened her robe and waited until Mitch noticed before sliding it off her shoulders to pool at her feet. Instantly his gaze flared hot, searing her flesh with his hungry look.

"I've got the plug in," she whispered, then ran her fingers across her hardened nipples.

Jake came up behind her and cupped her breasts, his naked body pressing against her back. He felt hot and further ignited her growing passions. Mitch watched, his gaze growing ever hotter as Jake licked at the side of her neck and massaged her aching breasts, his fingers pinching at her nipples.

Quickly throwing off his clothes, Mitch moved over and dropped to his knees before her. With a hand beneath her thigh, he lifted her leg and settled her foot against the stool close to the island. She leaned back against Jake, anxious for the feel of Mitch's wicked tongue sliding around her pussy. His thick, able fingers separated her labia and slid along her slit to the plug nestled in her ass. She moaned softly, bucking her hips outward toward his face. Gently he tugged on the plug, slowly sliding it in and out while his tongue licked along her wet pussy to draw teasing circles around her clit.

She gasped and buried one hand in Mitch's hair, trying to tug him closer. Every part of her body screamed for release, begged to be filled with his massive cock. Both of them. She wanted them both. Mitch pressed the flat of his tongue against her clit before sliding down to slip into her aching channel. Juices poured from her body, and Mitch moaned, licking away every drop that came forth.

"You taste so good, Tess," Mitch murmured against the inside of her thigh, and her whole body trembled.

"Mitch." She gasped, trying to pull his face back to her pussy.

"Want more, Tess?" he purred. "Do you want me to fuck you with my tongue again?"

"Yes."

His mouth returned to her pussy and she screamed. His warm tongue drew tantalizing circles around her swollen nub. Her hips bucked wildly as Jake's teeth continued to gently bite at the flesh of her neck. He rolled a hard nipple between his thumb and forefinger, causing her back to arch in a desperate plea for more.

"You're so beautiful, Tessa," Jake whispered in her ear. "I love watching your face as Mitch eats your pussy. Come for him, Tessa. Come down his throat while I watch."

Biting down on her lower lip, she ground her pussy as Mitch pressed the flat of his tongue against her clit. She exploded with a shout as her body rode wave after wave of intense pleasure. Her pussy throbbed, but an emptiness still ached through her channel. She needed to be fucked. Now—and hard.

"Please. One of you. I need to be fucked." Mitch thrust two fingers into her dripping channel, and she had to grab

Jake's arm to keep from falling. "Oh, God. Yes. Fuck me, Mitch."

Harder he thrust his fingers into her, but it still wasn't enough. She wanted more. "Please," she whispered.

Jake removed the plug and replaced it with two of his fingers. Both men moving together, one fucking her pussy, the other her ass. She couldn't take much more. Every muscle in her body quaked with a need far greater than any she'd felt before. She became mindless and undulated her body wildly, desperately clinging to her sanity.

"We both want to fuck you, Tessa," Jake purred. "Both of us at once."

"Yes." She gasped, surprised at just how badly she wanted it.

Jake removed his fingers and pressed his cock into the cleft of her ass. He was hot and thick, more than ready to fill her balls deep. Mitch stood as well, his erection tall and just as thick as Jake's. Truthfully, there wasn't much difference in them from the waist down. They were both magnificent.

Putting his hands under her hips, Mitch lifted her, helping her to settle her legs around his waist. Her pussy moved along his length, and Mitch's jaw clenched with barely contained control. Jake moved closer, the heat of his chest seeping into her back, sandwiching her between the two of them. Her heart raced in a split second of anxiety. Would it hurt? Or would it be incredible?

Slowly, Jake pressed his cock into her pussy from behind, stroking her pulsing channel and wetting his cock. Tessa gasped and moved with him, until he removed his shaft and moved his wet cock to the tight opening of her ass.

Gently, he pushed forward, stretching her with his huge cock. She held her breath, waiting for the bite of pain to subside and the pleasure to take over.

When he began to move, she groaned trying to press back against him so he would fuck her harder. Mitch continued to grind his cock along her slit, patiently waiting for what, she had no idea.

"Mitch?" She gasped, barely able to get the words out.

"When you want me, just say the word, Tess. I'm waiting for you."

"I want it," she screamed. "Oh, God. Please, Mitch."

Jake pulled almost out and waited for Mitch to position his shaft at her opening. They pushed forward together filling her beyond anything she'd ever felt before. At first, it was almost overwhelming and she stiffened. Both men stilled, their hearts beating a frantic rhythm, matching her own.

"Take a deep breath, Tess," Mitch instructed, and she did, slowly letting it out.

The two of them began to move with slow, shallow movements, giving her time to become accustomed to the sensation. With each thrust they went deeper and Tessa relaxed a little more. Her release built from deep inside her. The overwhelming sensation of both of them in her at once, the tantalizing spot they rubbed against as they moved as one, every touch of their lips and hands as they made love to her at the same time, sent her already sensitized nerves into a massive overdrive. Even their combined scents of musk and sex affected her.

"Harder," she whispered. "Harder, guys, please."

They obliged, thrusting harder and deeper into her passages. She panted, held immobile between them, but filled with so much searing pleasure she could hardly breathe. Her body convulsed as a wave of pleasure built within her core and sprang outward with alarming speed, taking the very breath from her lungs. Her anal muscles tightened around Jake, making him growl his approval. Her fingers dug into Mitch's shoulders as her body rode out the wave of bliss.

The two of them began to move in counterpoint, and her mouth fell open on a silent cry. Her legs trembled and tightened around Mitch's waist, holding tight as he rotated his hips slightly, grinding against her sensitive clit. With a cry, she exploded. Every part of her tingled, sparks ignited behind her eyes and she squeezed them shut, screaming as her release slammed through her.

"Fuck," Mitch growled. "It feels so damn good."

He tensed and shot his seed deep into her channel, pistoning his cock deep inside her. Jake followed a second later, his own shout of release ringing in her ears.

"Wow." She sighed as her body relaxed between them, shocked that orgasms could feel like that. "I think I like that."

Jake chuckled as Mitch covered her mouth with his. Her taste lingered on his lips and she licked at them, intrigued.

"I think I like that too." Mitch sighed into her mouth, and she smiled back at him.

Turning her head, she gave Jake a smile as well. His brown eyes held the same love and affection Mitch's held, and for a second, her chest tightened. “I love you both.” She sighed. “How am I going to choose?”

“Don’t worry about that right now, Tess,” Mitch said, a hint of sadness in his deep voice. “Just live in the moment. We’ll figure out the future later.”

* * *

Jake gently lowered her into the oversize tub. The water was warm and soothing, the bubbles soft and smelling of lavender. Her arms and legs were weak and hung like the limbs of a rag doll. Her eyes were half-closed, her mind already falling toward sleep.

Never in her life had she experienced an orgasm like that. Parts of her were tender, but her flesh still tingled from the intensity of her release and overrode any discomfort she might feel other places.

“Relax, baby,” Jake whispered, placing a soft kiss on her temple. “Let Mitch take care of you.”

“Where are you going?” she asked. Her hand reached out to cover his on the side of the tub.

“I’m going to finish dinner. I’m sure you’re hungry.”

“A little,” she admitted, a sheepish grin spreading her lips.

“Then maybe if you’re a good girl and eat well”—he taunted and brushed his fingers across her nipples, which immediately sprang to life—“Mitch and I will pleasure you again.”

Her teeth bit down on her lower lip, fighting the aroused tingle that shimmied down her spine. Just the idea of a repeat performance sent her body into a lust-filled state.

"Hurry with dinner," she whispered, and Jake grinned, placing another kiss on her cheek.

As he left her gaze turned to Mitch, who lit an arrangement of scented candles on the bathroom sink. Their light reflected in the mirror and cast a sensual glow around the darkened room. With a smile, she sank farther into the tub and let the water soothe her sated body.

"You look absolutely edible," Mitch said with a devilish grin.

"So do you," she purred.

Her gaze wandered down his wide chest and firm abs, straight to the impressive part of his body that had given her so much pleasure earlier. It hardened right before her eyes, the head of his thick cock coming to rest just under his belly button. His fist gripped the base and pumped upward. As she watched him, her heart sprang into a frantic rhythm and her pussy heated and tightened.

My God, what's wrong with me? I just had both of them and now I'm horny again?

But the sight of Mitch staring down at her, hunger blazing in his eyes as he stroked his cock, was too tempting to not affect her.

"Get in the tub with me," she ordered, and moved so Mitch could climb in behind her.

When he was settled, she moved to sit on his thighs. His hard cock pressed into the cleft of her ass, and she sighed, sagging back against his chest. They didn't speak, just cuddled. Mitch's warm breath fanned her neck as his hands gently brushed warm water up her arms and across her shoulders. Slowly, his touch became more arousing, more sensual.

Large palms reached around to cover her breasts, and she arched her back, her fingers digging into the flesh of his thighs. "What have you and Jake done to me?" she asked.

Inch by inch, one of his hands moved down to softly brush across her clit. She groaned and bit her lip. If she kept this up, her lips would be incredibly bruised and swollen.

"I think it's more what you've done to us," Mitch replied. "I can't seem to get enough of you."

His finger delved farther and slid along her slit, spreading the juices that had begun to pour from her pussy.

"Turn around, Tess," he whispered.

As quickly as possible, she turned, ignoring the slosh of water that fell over the side of the tub and onto the tile floor. She straddled his thighs and leaned forward to kiss his full, delectable mouth. His lips parted, allowing her tongue inside to explore and taste at her leisure. His hands skimmed up and down her back, then lower to grasp her hips and move her forward, position her over his straining cock.

Mitch was on fire. If he didn't get inside her soon, he'd fucking combust. What was this effect she had on him? All it took was a look and his cock sprang to immediate life, hardening to the point of bursting. The wet heat of her pussy moved along his length, and he groaned into her mouth. She tasted of strawberries and mint. Her toothpaste from earlier, maybe? He didn't care really. All he knew was that she tasted incredible and he couldn't get enough.

"Ah, Tess," he growled and bit a slow trail down the side of her neck to her breasts.

They were magnificent. Full and firm, and fit his hand perfectly. The rosy nipples were hard, begging for the flick of his tongue. Lifting one breast, he captured the pert tip in his mouth. Her back arched and her chest expanded on her sudden intake of breath.

He loved how she responded to him. How quickly she was ready to once again take his cock inside her tight pussy. His fingers moved between her legs and massaged along her slit. Even in the warm water, he could feel her heat, her readiness. She wanted him and he loved it.

"You're so wet, Tess." He moaned against her lips. "I can't wait to get my cock inside you again." Slowly he inserted two fingers and watched as her head fell back and her eyes closed on a moan. Her hips jerked, pulling his fingers deeper into her tight passage. "You're so fucking hot, Tess."

"Mitch," she said with a sigh. "I want you. Please."

"You want me, baby?" Mitch teased, finger fucking her with shallow thrusts.

"Yes," she growled and rotated her hips against his hand.

"Then take me. Take my cock inside you and fuck me, Tess."

Shoving his hand away, she straddled the head of his cock and pushed down hard. He groaned, thrusting his hips upward and embedding himself even deeper. She was so tight, so hot. It was like being encased in lava. Smooth, velvety lava.

"Oh, God. You feel so good, Tess."

Leaning forward, he captured one of her breasts with his mouth. Burying her hands in his hair, she tugged him closer, encouraging him to suckle harder. His teeth nipped at her nipple before moving lower and biting at the underside of her breast. She groaned, grinding her hips against him faster, forcing the water to slosh around them in rolling waves.

Grabbing her hips, he held her still and slightly up so he could pull almost out, then slowly thrust back in, letting her pussy slide along the full length of his aching cock.

"Oh, God." She sighed and gripped his shoulders as he did it again.

Over and over, he fucked her with long, slow strokes until neither of them could hold back any longer. With a hard thrust upward, he pulled down on her hips, then encouraged her to grind against him. Harder, faster, they moved as one until she exploded around him, her pussy pulsing and convulsing along his shaft. He groaned, fighting his own release until he'd wrung every last spasm out of her body. Just as her release subsided, he let loose his orgasm, his seed gushing into her tight body with wave on wave of pleasure.

"I love you, Tess." He sighed into her neck and held her tight.

She wrapped her arms around his neck, holding him in a death grip. He hated they were doing this to her, making her choose. He and Jake needed to talk. They had to work something out so they all won.

Chapter Eleven

Tessa bounded down the stairs, into the kitchen, and straight into Jake's arms. He grunted as she threw her arms around his neck and kissed him soundly. Chuckling, he kissed her back, his tongue licking along her bottom lip.

"What was that for?" he asked with a grin and circled her tiny waist with his arms.

"I don't know." She shrugged and smiled that adorable angelic smile that never failed to send his heart racing. "I just felt like it."

"Feel free to feel like that any time."

She laughed, and the sound floated around him to settle into his chest. God, he loved her and would always love her, no matter who she ended up with.

"Hey," Mitch grumbled as he came down the stairs to join them. "Where's dinner?"

"On the stove," Jake said as Tessa slipped from his arms. "Jealous?"

Mitch turned to stare at them with a thoughtful expression on his face. "You know, I'm not."

Tessa snorted and placed a bite of garlic bread in her mouth.

"Excuse me?" Mitch teased. "Was that a snort?"

"Yes," she replied. "You know, hearing you're not jealous is not exactly what a girl wants to hear."

"No?" Mitch chuckled. "So, what is it a woman wants to hear?"

"You're treading dangerous ground, friend," Jake murmured and carried the plates to the small table nestled within a bay window. Below them the lights of Gatlinburg twinkled in the darkness of the mountains.

Tessa crinkled her nose at Jake, making him smile.

"Women want to hear how the men who love them can't stand to see them with someone else."

"Well," Mitch said and leaned against the counter on the center island, his arms crossed over his chest. "Jake is different. For some reason, you touching Jake is like you're touching me."

"Now that just sounds weird," Jake said with a frown.

Tessa laughed. "No it doesn't. I think I actually understand."

"Then can you explain it to me? I'm not quite sure I do," Mitch said.

"Just grab the plates, ass," Jake growled, but the amusement in his eyes let them know he wasn't really aggravated.

Tessa picked up the basket of bread and placed it on the table with the rest of dinner—broiled chicken, steamed vegetables, and salad. Everything smelled wonderful, even if Jake did say so himself, and Jake didn't miss the sound of Tessa's stomach growling.

Placing her napkin in her lap, Tessa inhaled and smiled across the table at Jake. His heart pounded like a runaway horse galloping across the desert. The blue of her robe matched her eyes, making them appear darker and more intense.

"Everything smells wonderful," she said. "Keep cooking like this and I'll gain twenty pounds or more."

"Don't worry. We'll work it off you," Mitch replied with a wink.

An adorable blush moved up her neck, making her already rosy cheeks pinker. "The two of you are insatiable," she chided.

"Only for you," Jake purred, and her lips spread into a saucy little grin.

God, he wanted to throw her up on that table, forget the chicken, and have her for dinner instead. They needed to give her some time. After the ménage from earlier, and then the sex she and Mitch had in the tub, she was probably worn-out. Even though he hadn't said it, he'd agreed with what Mitch had said. The fact they'd had sex hadn't bothered him. Seeing her touch and kiss Mitch had felt natural. Like they'd been doing it this way all their lives.

"I was glancing through the television listings while dinner was cooking and the two of you were fooling around upstairs." With a wink toward Tessa, he continued. "There's a good horror moving coming on. Still like scary movies?"

"I love them," she said with a grin. "But I won't be able to sleep alone. I'll watch it only if the two of you sleep with me."

"All three of us in the same bed?" Mitch's eyes widened in mock shock. "Why Miss Tessa, what kind of man do you think I am?"

"The kind that will do anything to keep his woman happy," she countered and batted her eyelashes comically as she handed him the plate of steamed vegetables.

They all three laughed.

"I think it sounds like a great idea myself," Jake said with a smile, looking forward to later when Tessa was sandwiched between them, right where she belonged.

* * *

A finger poked at his shoulder and Jake opened one eye, glaring at Mitch over Tessa's shoulder. "What?" Jake whispered.

"Come downstairs," Mitch whispered back.

Jake frowned at his friend. What the hell was he up to at…he glanced at the clock by the massive king-sized bed they'd all crawled into after the movie earlier. It was three in the morning, for God's sake.

"I'm serious," Mitch growled softly.

Jake sighed and climbed from the bed as quietly as possible so not to wake Tessa. She was sleeping so soundly. Grabbing the covers, he settled them over her shoulders, then followed Mitch downstairs.

"What's going on?"

"Did you talk to the director?" Mitch asked.

"You woke me up to ask me that?"

Mitch scowled.

"Yes. I talked to him. Still nothing from her assistant, and now apparently her father has gone missing."

"What?"

"I didn't want to say anything earlier and upset Tessa." He pointed a finger at Mitch. "And don't you fucking say anything either."

"Does he think it's related to Admiral Shore's disappearance?"

"Yes."

"Damn," Mitch said with a sigh, dragging his hand through his short hair. "We need to talk about Tessa, Jake. It's why I originally called you down here."

Jake frowned, then moved to sit in the overstuffed chair by the now-cold fireplace. "All right. What about her?"

"I think this choosing thing is getting to her."

Jake nodded, wondering where this was going. "I agree."

"What do you think of…"

"Of what?"

"Not making her choose."

With a sigh, Jake scratched at his chin, almost dreading what he thought Mitch might be saying. "Are you saying you want us to choose instead?"

"No. I don't want any of us to have to choose."

Jake scowled as what Mitch implied finally registered. He'd thought of it himself before but dismissed it at the time. "What you're suggesting is illegal."

"I'm not suggesting bigamy, at least, not really. Only one of us would marry her legally, the other would just be there."

"And who would marry her legally?" His sarcastic tone wasn't lost on Mitch, who turned to scowl down at him.

"I'm getting to that. I think you should."

"I beg your pardon? You're actually handing her to me?"

"No," Mitch argued. "You're the wealthier of the two of us."

Jake shook his head. "What does that have to do with anything?"

"I have no family. You do. I can leave everything I have to Tessa, even if we're not married and there's no one to contest it."

"So you're basing this on the best way to make her financially secure if anything were to happen to us?"

"Yes. We don't exactly have the safest jobs in the world," Mitch said with a sigh.

"I'll agree with that. But do you really think we can make this work? I want kids, Mitch."

"So do I," Mitch said with a nod.

"Have you given any thought to how we would do that? Who would have kids first or do we just wing it, neither knowing which of us is the father?"

"That's not a bad idea," Mitch said with a shrug.

"It is for the kids," Jake cried in exasperation. "Have you even thought this through at all?"

"Yes, damn it, I have."

Mitch began to pace the room, his hand dragging through his hair again, a sure sign he was agitated. "There are aspects that would have to be worked out, that's a given. As far as kids, we can go by age. You're older, therefore you and Tessa have one first."

"You're out of your mind," Jake said with a shake of his head.

"This is the best idea and you know it."

Jake sighed and placed his hand over his mouth, his mind playing out the possibilities. It would certainly solve their problem, but how would Tessa feel about it? How would she react if they even brought it up?

"Don't bring this up to Tessa yet," Jake said, and Mitch nodded his head in agreement. "Let's work on her a little first. Warm her up to the idea slowly."

"Show her what it would be like to always have both of us?"

"Yeah," Jake said with a slight quirk to his lips. Maybe they could make this work after all.

* * *

"Wake up, sleepyhead," Jake purred in her ear, making her skin prickle in desire.

"Mmmm," she murmured, stretching lazily. The stinging slap to her hip made her jump and come awake instantly. "Ouch," she cried and rubbed at the spot Jake had spanked.

Jake chuckled down at her. "We're taking you to town today, remember?"

"Oh yeah." She sighed, still not wanting to move from the comfort of the bed.

"Well, woman. Up and at 'em."

"Okay, okay," she grumbled as she slowly climbed from bed and headed toward the shower. "I'd forgotten just how damn bossy you were."

"Excuse me?" Jake asked, trying to sound offended, but failing miserably.

"You heard me. I said *bossy*," she snapped back, sticking her head out the door for a split second before slamming it shut.

Jake snickered and grabbed a sweater from the open suitcase on the floor. Mitch was downstairs making coffee, and Jake was tempted to join Tessa in the shower, but figured they'd worn the poor woman out enough. But it wouldn't hurt to tease her a little, he thought with a grin as he softly opened the bathroom door and stepped inside.

Steam already filled the room, for Tessa liked her showers scalding. The scent of her lavender soap hung in the air and he inhaled deeply remembering that same smell on her flesh as she'd slept close to him last night. Stepping softly, he walked over to the shower and opened the glass door.

She hadn't noticed him. Her head was back, her eyes closed as she rinsed the shampoo from her hair, totally unaware of his presence. He reached out, his finger heading straight for the puckered nipple of her breast, when her amused voice stopped him cold.

"Don't even think about it."

He glanced up and smiled. She watched him, her eyes narrowing to tiny blue slits.

"Oh, honey. I was about to do more than just think about it," he drawled playfully.

Her lips lifted into a sexy half smile. "You and Mitch are absolutely insatiable."

"So are you telling me that if I wanted you right now, you'd say no?"

"Are you saying you want me right now?" she countered.

"I don't know. Are you saying no?"

She laughed and splashed water toward him, dampening his gray sweater. "You know I could never say no to either one of you."

Jake smiled. She was so adorable, and at times, so young at heart. That childlike enthusiasm was what he'd loved most about her. That and her body. His gaze traveled down her curvy figure stopping at the light sprinkling of hair just above her pussy. Feeling devilish, he reached out and drew his finger along her slit, making her gasp. With one long thrust, he entered her pussy, pushing his finger knuckle deep before pulling it back out again.

His gaze never left hers as he slid that same finger into his mouth, sucking at her juices. She tasted just like heaven. "Mmmm," he murmured. "Just to tide me over."

"You're terrible," she growled. "Out! Before I give you a little taste of your own medicine."

She grabbed the door handle and pulled it shut. Through the fogged glass he could see her turn her back, and he chuckled, knowing she wasn't really angry.

"Tease me, baby," he pleaded above the sound of running water.

The sponge she'd used came flying over the top of the shower door, just missing him as he dodged out of the way. Laughing, he quickly left the bathroom before her aim improved.

* * *

"This is cute," Tessa said and held up a white T-shirt with airbrushed lettering. "'I'm not bald. It's a solar panel for a sex machine.'"

Jake raised an eyebrow while Mitch snorted. Tessa giggled at both of them. They'd had such an incredible day. The weather had been warm, even for the mountains, and they'd taken advantage, spending most of the day going through the multitude of shops along the main strip.

Both men had been incredibly attentive and affectionate. Matter of fact, they were spoiling her. How could a woman go back to just dating one man after spending days being showered with attention by these two? She frowned, placing the T-shirt back on the rack.

"What's wrong, Tess?" Mitch whispered, his hand gently rubbing up and down her back.

"I was just thinking how much fun it's been today and how much I wish it could always be like this."

"Who says it can't?"

She turned to stare at him in confusion. They couldn't keep this up. That was ridiculous.

"You know what, Tess? Don't think about it. Just live for the moment and worry about tomorrow later. Let Jake and me show you how much we love you."

"I know how much you love me," she whispered. "And that's part of what bothers me."

"Don't." He leaned down and placed a soft kiss on her lips. "Remember. Happy thoughts."

A small smile tugged at her lips. "Happy thoughts," she agreed and let Mitch lead her from the shop to join Jake at the small coffeehouse next door.

Jake stood at the counter, eyeing row after row of fudge. Tessa came up behind him, enjoying the view of his firm ass in the jeans he wore. Wrapping her arm around his waist, she smiled up at him as he slid his arm around her shoulders.

"So which will it be, sunshine? Rocky Road or Double Dutch Chocolate?"

"Why not live on the edge and get both?" she asked with a grin.

Jake winked back with a smile, his brown eyes sparkling with happiness and humor. "Why not." Turning back to the girl at the counter, he placed an order for the Rocky Road, Chocolate, and a block of peanut butter for Mitch.

With fudge and coffee in hand, they stepped outside to sit at the numerous wrought-iron tables lining the sidewalk. Mitch had stepped down the street into one of the many shops, but Tessa wasn't sure which. He'd just told them he'd be back in a few.

As they waited, they sipped their coffee and fed each other fudge. Tessa couldn't remember the last time she was this happy. Or this content. There was definitely something to be said about dating two men at once.

"Enjoying yourself?" Jake asked, a teasing grin spreading his lips.

The cool breeze ruffled his hair, and she brushed a lock away from his forehead.

"I'm having a blast."

"Mitch and I aren't overwhelming you?" Concern made his eyes crinkle, and she placed her hand over the one he had lying on the table.

"No," she said quietly, then smiled.

Jake opened his mouth to speak, but his cell phone rang, interrupting whatever he was about to say. He pulled it from his pocket and glanced at the caller ID. "It's the director," he said as he flipped it open. "Yeah."

Tessa tried to hear what was said on the other end, but couldn't. Biting her nails, she waited for Jake to finish and hopefully give her some news.

"Well?" she asked as Jake flipped the phone closed.

"Sparks has a lead, and he'll meet up with us later."

"A lead?" She let out the breath she didn't even realize she was holding. "What lead?"

"Apparently, it's your father. He found out who the leak is."

She wished she still had her cell phone. Had her father tried to text her to tell her the name of the person behind it all? A frown pulled at Jake's forehead, and it caused her own nerves to stand on end. "What's wrong? It's almost over, right?"

"Not yet. Your father still has to work with Sparks and tell him what he knows. He did confirm there's someone on the inside, but your father thinks there're more involved than just the NCIS agent."

"Someone in the military?"

"Possibly. We'll have to give Sparks time to put it all together."

"What about Kate?" she asked. Tessa still had a hard time with the fact that Kate had planted the tracers. Surely they were wrong.

"He has a tail on her, but they haven't confronted her yet. They don't want to tip anyone off just in case she's still in contact with them. So far, though, they haven't seen anything to indicate she is."

"Good. I think. I still can't believe she would do something like that."

"I know," Jake said and placed a soft kiss on her cheek. "Try not to think about it."

"I can't help it. She was my friend. I can't believe I would be that stupid."

"You're not stupid, Tessa." Jake gave her a firm look, silently indicating there would be no argument on that.

Over his shoulder, she noticed Mitch coming down the sidewalk. He'd covered his T-shirt with a denim jacket that made his shoulders look even wider, matching jeans hugged his lean hips. She couldn't stop staring at him, at the way he sauntered so confidently. His blue eyes met hers and he winked. He was such a sexy devil.

Grabbing a chair, he turned it backward so he could straddle the seat on the other side of Tessa. She liked being between them like this. It always made her feel protected and safe.

"What are you all smiles about?" she asked.

"I saw you," he countered, making her snicker.

"You're so full of it," she teased.

"Yeah, but you love me," he drawled.

Tessa laughed.

"We heard from Sparks," Jake said, interrupting their conversation.

Mitch was immediately all business and ignored the fudge Jake passed over to him. "What did he say?"

"Tessa's father contacted him. He knows who the leak is."

Mitch nodded and opened the paper surrounding the fudge. "Good."

Breaking off a piece, he popped it into this mouth and sighed, his eyes closing in sheer delight. Tessa couldn't take her eyes off him. He had almost the same expression on his face when he came.

"Is it good?" she asked, her voice cracking with amusement.

"Oh yeah. Almost as good as you." Mitch reached into his pocket and pulled out a narrow, flat box. "I have something for you."

Tessa's eyes widened in shock. "Mitch, you didn't have to get me anything."

"I know. I wanted to. It's actually a reminder of our time together."

With shaking fingers she took the box and flipped it open. Inside was a gold bracelet with three hearts entwined together. "It's beautiful." She sighed and lifted the delicate piece of jewelry from the box.

Mitch took it and secured it around her wrist. "The heart in the middle represents you. Always surrounded and protected by us."

She smiled and cupped his face with her hands, pulling him to her for a gentle kiss. "I love it. Thank you."

Mitch smiled and kissed her forehead, making tears well up in her eyes. Her heart ached so much whenever she thought about having to choose. Why did she have to? Why couldn't she have them both?

"That is nice," Jake said as he studied the bracelet. "I may have to kiss you myself."

"The hell you will," Mitch grumbled and slid his chair back from the table. The iron scraped against the concrete, sending chills up Tessa's back. The sound was like someone scraping their nails along a chalkboard. But she couldn't stop the giggle that spewed forth at the horrified expression on Mitch's face.

"You know, that's kind of an interesting image," Tessa said and batted her eyelashes at each of them.

"I'm willing to try a lot of things, Tessa. But that's not one of them," Jake said, his lips quirking in amusement.

"No? Where's your sense of adventure?" she teased.

"Buried," Mitch growled. "I may love him like a brother, but *not* a lover. Sorry, Jake, but you're just not my type."

Jake snorted, sticking his middle finger in the air toward Mitch. Tessa laughed so hard her eyes welled up. No doubt about it. These two were a blast.

Chapter Twelve

Jake spread the blanket on the hardwood floor in front of the fireplace and poked at the embers, bringing the fire back to life. A late-season snowstorm had moved through in the last hour, taking everyone by surprise and blanketing the mountainside in a growing layer of white.

Tessa had stood at the window watching it fall, the serene smile on her face making his chest tighten. She loved watching it snow, and seeing her like that had brought back memories of the last time they'd watched the snow fall.

Mitch strolled over, slinging his shirt across the back of the chair and placed a platter of cheese in the center of the blanket, along with three wineglasses.

"Red or white?" Mitch asked.

Jake looked at him in confusion until his question registered. "Oh…um…sorry. Red."

Mitch smiled and held up a bottle of red wine. Jake shook his head in amusement, then glanced back at Tessa who had turned to watch them with smoldering heat shining in her eyes.

"Go put on that outfit we bought, Tess," Mitch suggested.

She turned to him and grinned wickedly. "The blue one with the…" Her hands came up to brush across her breasts and Jake swallowed.

"Yeah, that one," Mitch said with a grin.

"The what?" Jake asked in exasperation.

"You'll see," she teased, then turned to head upstairs and change.

"Personally, I would be just as happy if she came down here nude," Jake said with a snicker.

Mitch set the bottle on the floor by the glasses. "Yeah, but it's so much more fun when we get to undress her."

Jake's cock began to harden just thinking about it. Unbuttoning his shirt, he threw it across the chair over Mitch's. Here with his best friend since childhood, preparing to make incredible love with the only woman he'd ever loved felt right. It was amazing how she'd taken to the two of them, accepting both of them together or separately and showing them all the love she had in her. She was amazing, and every day he fell a little more in love, which he was amazed was even possible.

"We should talk to her tonight, Mitch," Jake said with a sigh.

"Why tonight?"

"What if she doesn't agree to this? The three of us in a marriage."

Mitch was silent for several minutes before he spoke. "I think if we talk to her too soon, she'll balk at the idea. We should spend more time with her as a threesome, get her used to it."

"I think she's already used to it," Jake replied in a hushed voice.

"She's warmed over to the sex, but..."

Mitch stopped and glanced toward the stairs. Jake turned as well and sucked in a breath at the beautiful sight greeting him. She stood halfway down, a light blue satin baby-doll teddy covering her curvy torso. The top barely covered her breasts, and the bra support pushed them together, showing everything except her rosy nipples. Her legs were bare and long, and Jake grinned as soon as he saw the matching high-heeled sandals.

"Damn, Tessa," he growled. "You look fabulous."

She smiled and let her fingers softly trail down the banister as she stepped to the bottom. Her hair was loose and gathered around her shoulders in soft curls, her blue eyes sparkling with excitement and desire. Licking her lips, her stare moved to Mitch, who held out his hand indicating she should join him on the blanket.

Jake watched, unable to move as she stepped into Mitch's arms. Reaching up, she wrapped her arms around his neck and slanted her lips across his. Mitch kissed her back, his hands moving lower to grip her bare ass beneath the flimsy material of the baby-doll outfit.

Mitch broke the kiss and turned her to face Jake. "Kiss her, Jake," Mitch whispered.

Jake stepped forward and lowered his lips to hers. She moaned and opened her mouth, allowing his tongue to slide inside. Her fingers moved lower, brushing across his hard cock through the coarse material of his pants. If he didn't stop this and get himself more under control, he'd fuck her right now. Forget the foreplay.

He pulled away, trying to ignore Tessa's whimper of protest. Placing a finger over her lips, he gently pushed her to the blanket and handed her a glass of wine. Jake and Mitch both removed their pants, settling naked next to her. The heat of the fire felt good against their naked flesh and turned Tessa's golden in the light of the flames. Reaching out, he traced the edge of the lace bra, letting his finger trail across her soft skin.

She smiled and sipped at her glass, her gaze moving to follow his finger as it trailed along the material. He dipped it lower, brushing across her nipple, and she gasped, arching her chest out slightly.

"You know what would taste incredible with this wine?" Jake whispered.

"No," she said with a shake of her head. "What?"

"You." With a twist of his finger, he pushed the material lower, freeing one of her breasts from the tight confines of the bra.

Her nipple beaded beneath his stare as he gently rubbed wine across the tip. Lowering his head, he licked at her wine-covered flesh. She moaned, burying her hand in his hair to pull him closer. His cock throbbed to be inside her and feel her pussy rippling along his length.

His kisses worked up her neck, stopping to nibble behind her ear. "Do you have any idea what I want to do to you? How bad I want to fuck you? To lick your pussy and taste your juices as you come in my mouth?"

Tessa shivered, imagining Jake's tongue as he gently slid it along her wet slit. The wine burned through her veins as she fought hard to keep from throwing Jake to the floor and riding his thick cock. Mitch was behind her, his hands softly moving up the outside of her thigh, his lips nibbling along the back of her shoulder. Shifting, he moved to his knees.

"Sit on my lap, Tess," he whispered.

Climbing over his knees, she settled her bottom against his rock-hard shaft. Mitch moaned as she wiggled against him playfully.

"Be still, minx," he growled.

She stilled and waited with shallow breaths as Mitch slid her skirt up and spread her thighs, exposing her pussy to Jake's hungry view. Jake dribbled wine over her lower stomach and let it trail down and onto her slit. She gasped as he reached out with his finger, spreading the wine and mixing it with her own juices.

With one hand, Mitch reached around and freed her other breast, allowing him to play with both her nipples. Her senses were on overload. Every part of her body burned and pulsed, begging for fulfillment. One of Jake's fingers thrust into her pussy, and her hips jerked outward, wanting more.

"Oh, yes." She sighed.

Slowly he withdrew his finger, then placed it between her lips. The musky taste of her juices blended with the sweet taste of the wine, and she sucked at his knuckle, getting every drop. His eyes bored into hers, scorching her with their intensity and heat. Mitch's cock rocked into the cleft of her ass, setting a slow rhythm that made her wild.

She watched in fascination as Jake lowered his head and drew his tongue along her slit. She hissed, trying to grab a handful of his hair and shove his face into her aching mound. She was tired of the teasing, she wanted to come, but Jake or Mitch would have none of that. Mitch grabbed her hands, holding them firmly at her sides.

A groan tore from her throat as Jake slowly circled her clit with his tongue before sliding lower and dipping into her channel. It felt so good. She loved how his tongue delved and flicked, how his hot breath brushed across her clit. She shuddered and ground her hips, moving against both Jake's face and Mitch's cock.

Panting, her hands fisted and her nails dug into the palms of her hands. She couldn't hold back any longer, and with a shout, lost her hold on her control. Her body shook with each throb of her pussy against Jake's face. He groaned, licking away every drop of cream that spewed forth. Mitch's soft voice cooed words of praise into her ear, telling her how beautiful she was, how much he wanted her.

Gently, they lowered her to the floor, her body still weak and tingling. Jake touched his lips to hers in a gentle kiss, but Tessa wanted none of that. Forcing her tongue into his mouth, she kissed him with wild abandon, letting him know without words how she felt. How much she loved and wanted him.

Mitch used his fingers to spread her labia and gently blew his hot breath against her pulsing mound. She gasped, pulling away from Jake's kiss.

"Sensitive?" Mitch asked, as he flicked his tongue around her clit, barely touching her.

"Yes." She sighed and bit down on her lower lip.

Her stomach tightened as Jake again poured wine down her stomach and between her legs. With a grin, he also poured some over her breasts then leaned down to lick his tongue along her flesh. Tessa closed her eyes with a groan as pleasure and desire began to build within her body.

Mitch nipped at her nether lips, teasing her by licking and kissing everywhere except her sensitive clit. She could feel it swell and throb with each swipe of his tongue as it got closer and closer, then only to retreat and dip into her wet vagina. Her arms floated above her head and her hands grabbed two handfuls of the blanket beneath her. She could hardly breath as Mitch and Jake continued to feast on her body, making her wild and so damn turned on.

The flames from the fire burned against her already overheated flesh, and a thin sheen of perspiration broke out along her skin. Jake moved to circle her nipple with his tongue, teasing her aching mounds. Over and over, he circled until she arched her back, begging him to take it in his mouth. Ignoring her plea, he licked the flat of his tongue across her hard nub, and she gasped loudly, digging her nails deeper into the blankets.

She was now beyond coherent thought as the two continued to lick and tease her body. Bucking wildly, she ground her hips against Mitch's face until he put his hand on her hip to hold her still. She fought against him, groaning softly for more of his sweet torture. Heaven help her; if they didn't stop, she'd come again. She was so close.

Jake began to suck her breasts in earnest, pulling as much of the mound as he could into his mouth. Mitch followed by sliding two fingers deep into her channel and suckling on her clit. She instantly lost it. Her body exploded into another wave of pleasure so strong and so intense she cried out, her eyes filling with unshed tears.

Her pussy clamped down on Mitch's fingers as he pushed them in and out, fucking her hard and deep. Every thrust of his hand brought her hips off the blanket as she rode out her release. Still riding out her high, Jake turned her to her side where Mitch shifted to lie behind her, Jake at her front. Lifting her leg, Jake settled it over his arm allowing Mitch to drive his cock deep into her pussy.

She screamed, arching her back to meet his slow, deep thrusts. "Yes." She sighed, digging her nails into Jake's shoulder.

His hard cock pressed into her stomach as Mitch fucked her from behind, his thick cock filling her aching channel. She could feel the heat rising again, the pressure building as her body pulsed in rapture. Jake's mouth captured hers, swallowing her whimpers of delight. His tongue plundered and teased, taking everything she had to give and asking for more. He tasted of wine and smelled of burning wood and sex. The combination was almost as heady as his kisses.

Mitch pulled out and positioned his now-wet cock at the opening of her anus. Gently, he pushed forward, filling her with his thick shaft. She closed her eyes and moaned, lifting her leg higher in order to take him deeper. Jake rubbed the tip of his shaft around her clit, making her shudder.

"Damn it, Jake. Do it." She gasped, desperate for the feel of both of them within her body.

With a hard thrust, he pushed deep, taking the air from her lungs. She gasped for air, then sighed as they both pulled almost out, then pushed back in with one smooth movement.

Their moans and grunts mingled, each lost in the feel of the other. Tessa felt so loved and protected, sandwiched between them like she was. Jake at her front, Mitch at her back. Both of them making love to her so sweetly, so tenderly, she ached all over with the love she felt for them.

Tears streamed down her face as the tension in her body grew. Jake kissed at them, licking them away with his tongue. "Shhh, don't cry. Are we hurting you, Tessa?" Jake whispered.

"No," she shook her head, swallowing down a sob. "It feels so good."

They moved faster, their hard thrusts timed in perfect unison. Mitch nibbled along her neck and shoulder while Jake nipped at her jawline. She jerked and bucked as her pussy and anus began to pulse, pulling them deeper.

"Tessa," Mitch growled. "You feel so damn good."

"Oh, God. Like this, she's so fucking tight," Jake growled, then licked at her lower lip. "Come for us, Tessa. I can feel you're close. Your pussy is so tight and hot. It feels so good when it ripples along my length, when it clamps down on me like a hot vise."

She gulped in air as her pussy did just that and rippled along his hard length. Even the muscles of her anus tightened, clamping down on Mitch and making him groan in pleasure. Harder and deeper they pounded into her, and she screamed, riding out the waves of her release in stunned surprise as she tightened and shuddered along their cocks.

With a shout of their own, they came with her, each spilling their seed deep into her body along with a little piece of their souls.

Jake rained kisses along her jaw as Mitch kissed her neck. Their hands ran down her body in soothing motions. She had no idea how long they stayed like that, wrapped in each other's arms. She wasn't aware of much of anything until Mitch lifted her into his arms and headed upstairs to the deep Jacuzzi tub in the master bedroom.

Gently, he laid her in the warm water filled with lavender bubbles. Instantly her body relaxed, trusting her two men to take care of her. The last thing she remembered was being softly washed, one man on each side.

"I love you both so much," she whispered before falling into a deep, contented sleep.

* * *

Admiral Williams stepped out of his car slowly, his eyes squinting against the hot Hawaiian sun. Something didn't feel right about this. He could feel it deep in his gut and his gut never lied. He'd texted Tessa, but had not gotten a response, and he'd spent the better part of the day convincing himself not to worry. Easier said than done, unfortunately, especially after the message he'd received from Sparks.

He implied his daughter was in danger, unless he agreed to meet. He'd agreed, but not before sending all the information he had to his contact at JAG with strict orders that if he hadn't heard from him in twenty-four hours to take care of it.

Williams had chosen this public place deliberately, just in case there was any trouble. He didn't want to believe Sparks would do this, but there were too many red flags, too much evidence pointing to his friend. He had to keep his guard up. It was in his military nature and probably always would be.

Across from him, a Dodge Durango pulled into the empty lot, and Director Sparks stepped from the vehicle. Williams tensed, waiting.

"Admiral," Sparks acknowledged from about fifteen feet away with a nod of his head.

Williams nodded. "Where's my daughter?"

"She's safe. I think you and I should talk. Don't you?" Sparks said and took a couple of steps closer.

"You're not in this alone, are you Sparks?" Williams asked.

Sparks walked closer and grinned. Something about the evil hint to his smile put Williams on edge. "I don't know what you're talking about, Admiral. We really shouldn't discuss this here." He waved his hand toward the Durango. "Perhaps somewhere more private?"

It would be a foolish thing to do, but at the moment, he didn't have a whole lot of choice. He needed to find out where his daughter was.

Williams climbed into the back seat, staring with narrowed eyes at the man smiling back at him through the rearview mirror. Scott. General Scott Folks. "How many others are there, Sparks? Just how high up does this go?"

Sparks just shot him an amused grin, and Williams knew he'd be getting no answers from him. At least not yet.

"I think it's time you and I go see your daughter, Admiral," Sparks replied. "I want to make sure you do exactly what we need you to do."

Chapter Thirteen

Tessa awoke to the smell of coffee and burning wood. Glancing around, she spotted the fire burning in the bedroom fireplace. Gray light spilled across the wooden floors. She looked out the large pane window overlooking the mountains and took in the snow-covered trees. It still fell, thickening the layer that already clung to the ground.

It was cold in the room, and she shivered beneath the heavy quilt. Pulling it up tighter under her chin, she glanced around the bed, realizing she was alone. The guys must be downstairs.

The guys, she thought with a sigh. How could she choose? She loved them both with all her heart. The idea of hurting one of them made her physically ill, but the idea of never having either of them made her feel worse.

Oh, God. What am I supposed to do?

Last night had been so incredible, so exciting. If only things could always be like that.

I have to talk to them. I have to tell them I want them both.

Just as she thought about getting out of bed to go join the men, Mitch came into the room. The navy blue sweater deepened the shade of his eyes, and the corners crinkled as he smiled at her. "Morning, gorgeous. Dress warm, the power is out."

"Really? No wonder it's so cold in here."

Mitch nodded and grabbed a pair of jeans and sweater from the closet for her to put on. "As soon as Jake realized it, he started the fires. Good thing there's plenty of wood."

"How are we going to cook?" she asked as she reached for the bra she'd left on the floor the night before.

"The stove is gas. You can light it with a match. You can't light the oven, but the burners work. Hungry?" he asked, his gaze watching her carefully.

"Starving." She sighed.

"Tessa?"

She turned to look at him and smiled sadly. Unable to keep it inside any longer, she blurted out her feelings. "I can't do it, Mitch."

He stepped closer and clasped her shoulders in a gentle hold. "Do what?"

"Choose."

Tears streamed down her face in earnest. Biting her lip, she tried to keep it from trembling. The last thing she wanted was to blubber like an idiot through this.

"Oh, Tess." Mitch sighed and cupped her face with his hands. "Look at me."

Sniffing back a sob, she met his sweet, understanding gaze. It was so full of love, her heart ached. She loved him so much. Always had. "What am I going to do?" she sobbed. "I love you both. I can't pick. Mitch. I just can't."

Mitch pulled her into his arms and held her tight. She crumbled, letting all the pent-up emotions escape. Her fingers dropped the bra she had in her hand and clung to his shirt, as she cried out her despair into his chest. His heart beat softly beneath her cheek, and the slow rise and fall of his chest comforted her. Mitch was her rock, a small piece of the whole the three of them created together.

Mitch without Jake or vice versa didn't feel right. It would be like they were missing a part of themselves.

"It's going to be okay, Tess. I promise," Mitch crooned as his hand gently smoothed down her hair.

"How can it be?" she cried.

"What's wrong with Tessa?" Jake asked as he came into the room.

His voice was full of concern, and she glanced at him with eyes full of more unshed tears. Pulling away from Mitch she ran toward Jake and threw herself into his arms. One arm tightened around her waist, while the other hand held the back of her head against his chest.

"What happened?" he asked over her head to Mitch.

"She's upset about choosing."

"Didn't you tell her?" Jake demanded.

"I was about to."

"About to tell me what?" Tessa asked as she wiped at the wetness on her cheeks.

"You don't have to choose, Tessa," Jake began. "You can have both of us."

She gaped, her eyes widening in shock and confusion. "What?"

"We both love you and you love both of us. There's no reason we can't make this work," Mitch reasoned.

Tessa moved away from them to sit on the bed. She'd just been thinking about this same thing, but now that it might actually be a possibility, she wasn't as sure. She wanted both of them, so it wasn't that. It was the logistics of it all. How could they make this work? How would she explain this to people?

I have two husbands. I sleep with them both.

Well, that's ridiculous. It wasn't anyone's business, so why would she even have to explain anything to anyone? Her father. Oh, God. How would she explain something like this to him?

She raised a hand and began to bite at her fingernail, her mind running through all the possibilities of this scenario. And children. What about children?

"Tessa?" Jake whispered.

She glanced up and caught the two of them watching her expectantly. "I'm sorry," she said.

"Sorry?" Mitch croaked. "Sorry for what?"

She shook her head. "For zoning out, I guess. Are the two of you serious? Do you really think we can make something like that work?"

"Mitch and I have been all through it. I think we've worked out everything, including children."

"You guys want kids?" she asked, her heart soaring, but at the same time, her mind reeling.

"Yes," they replied in unison, and Tessa smiled, imagining a daughter with Jake's coloring and a son with

Mitch's. Even vice versa, she didn't care. All that mattered was she didn't have to make a gut-wrenching choice.

Jumping from the bed, she threw herself into Mitch's arms and kissed him soundly. He chuckled and kissed her back. His arms wrapped around the small of her back, lifting her so her feet dangled off the floor. Breaking the kiss, she turned her head and grabbed the collar of Jake's shirt, tugging him to her for a kiss. With a smile, he nipped at her lower lip and slapped at her hip softy.

"Get dressed, baby. Breakfast is cooking on the stove, and you're entirely too tempting in nothing," Jake teased.

She licked her lips, her body already burning for the touch of their hands. But they all needed to talk. She wanted to know how they'd worked this out. "I'll be down in a minute," she said with a smile.

Jake gave her one final quick peck on the lips, then turned to leave the room. Mitch lingered behind, his gaze watching her as she slowly dressed. "You make me crazy when you do that," she said as she eyed Mitch through her lashes.

"When I do what?" he asked, his eyes crinkling in mischief as he reclined on the mattress.

His forearm flexed beneath the sweater as he leaned on his elbow and crossed his ankles. He was such a hot specimen and he knew it. The blue of his eyes darkened as she straightened, deliberately stretching her arms above her head and thrusting out her breasts before leaning over to grab the sweater off the bed. She didn't really need it. The desire in Mitch's eyes warmed her body enough to make her break out in a sweat.

"Just imagine, Tess. You'll be able to dress and tease Jake and me for the rest of our lives."

"At least until I get all old and wrinkled," she teased.

"You'll still be beautiful," he replied with a smile, and her heart melted even more.

"What if we have a daughter and she wants to do something like this?" she asked.

"You mean marry two men?"

"Yeah." She pulled the sweater over her head and tugged it down around her waist.

"I would be happy with whatever made her happy. Of course, I say that now, but when the time comes I'm sure I'll be an old conservative fart who can't see his daughter having sex with one man much less two."

Tessa laughed and tugged her jeans over her hips and snapped them closed. "There's a lot of stuff to work out," she said with a sigh.

"We can do it, Tess. Jake and I have already gone through a lot of it."

"What if I don't like what you guys have come up with?"

He pursed his lips with a nod. "Well, then, we'll listen to what you have to say, consider it, then you'll do as Jake and I say."

With a growl, she threw a pillow at him, making him laugh.

"In your dreams, Agent Robbins."

"Hey," he snarled and grabbed her wrist, tugging her down on the bed with him, then rolling over, pinning her beneath his hard body. "That's husband number two to you, woman."

"Oh, I see what this is going to be like," she said playfully as Mitch drew her hands up over her head, pinning them to the mattress.

"What?" he teased.

His hot breath fluttered across her lips, making her shiver.

"The both of you are too bossy for words."

Mitch chuckled and placed a soft kiss on her lips. "As much as I would love to continue this conversation, I think we better get downstairs and eat breakfast before the bossiest one of all of us comes barreling up here."

Tessa smiled. "I love you, Mitch."

"I know," he drawled with a grin. Tessa groaned and rolled her eyes heavenward.

* * *

Tessa sank farther into the outdoor hot tub, letting the warm water and steam relax the tension from her body. The snow had stopped falling and the power had been restored, but they hadn't yet cleared off the road. Jake thought it might be a while, since they were so far up the mountain.

Which, in all honesty, was fine by her. She enjoyed being alone with her men. *Her men*, she thought with a smile.

Life would certainly be interesting. Two men always around, always taking care of her. She liked the idea.

Glancing around, she noticed Mitch to her left. His head was back as he stared up toward the snow-covered trees towering over their deck. Blue sky peeked through the clouds, hinting at the beautiful day to follow.

Jake was to her right. His eyes were closed as he leaned his head back against the side of the tub. He looked so relaxed. Was he asleep? He'd told her over breakfast that he and Mitch had been up most of the night discussing their plan and working out all the details. They'd certainly covered everything, right down to who would have kids first.

Could they really make this work?

Turning her head, she studied Mitch's stubble and strong jaw. He was so handsome, so masculine and rugged. She and Jake would be the ones to officially marry. Would Mitch be tired of always, in a sense, being the third wheel? Would he get tired of sharing her and eventually want a wife of his own?

The thought of losing him to someone else made her stomach tie in knots, and she didn't even want to think of him with another woman. It made her feel as though she were dying inside. God, how did he and Jake do it? Did it not bother them to see her with the other? They swore it didn't, but how could it not?

"What's that frown for, sunshine?" Mitch asked softly.

She glanced in confusion toward his smiling eyes. "I was frowning?"

He nodded and wiped a stray lock of hair from her eyes.

"I was just thinking," she whispered.

"About?"

"The three of us. It would kill me to see you with someone else, but you and Jake seem to handle it fine. Do you really or are you just telling me that so I won't worry?"

A soft smile tugged at Mitch's lips. "You have nothing to worry about, Tess. I promise. It doesn't bother me to see you have sex with Jake. Matter of fact"—he leaned forward and grabbed her wrist, tugging her toward him—"I think I know just how to prove it to you."

"And how's that?" she asked as she stood before Mitch, her breasts high and firm. His gaze wandered down her body, heating her already pink flesh.

"Fuck Jake while I watch."

"What?" she asked, shock momentarily stilling her breathing.

"I think that's a great idea," Jake said from behind her, and she turned to stare at him over her shoulder.

Glancing back toward Mitch, she asked. "So you're just going to sit there and watch while Jake and I have sex?"

"Maybe for a while, then maybe I'll join in." His grin sent her heart racing wildly.

"All right," she answered, grinning back at him. She would make it her personal challenge to test his will—see how long he could only watch before he lost control.

Putting her back to him, she spun around to face Jake. A cold breeze blew, making her nipples pucker, and Jake smiled, licking his tongue across his lips seductively.

"I like your breasts, Tessa," he purred. "Come here so I can taste them."

With deliberate slowness, Tessa moved toward him, close enough that he could reach out and squeeze her aching breasts with his palm. She moaned, arching her back as he gently massaged her heavy mounds. He put his hand at the small of her back, pulling her closer so he could lift her breasts with his other hand and circle her nipple with the tip of his tongue. She groaned, wanting to feel the heat of his mouth envelop her, and when he did, she gasped desperately for air.

She no longer noticed the cold as Jake continued to tease and torment her with his hands and mouth. Glancing behind her, she noticed Mitch watching them. His heated gaze took in every curve and undulation of her body. Jake's hand slid between her legs and cupped her pussy. Heat consumed her as he softly stroked her flesh, ever so slowly separating her folds to fondle her opening. Her hips jerked forward, wanting him to dip his fingers inside her depths, but he held off and kept teasing her.

"Lick her pussy, Jake," Mitch ordered.

Jake lifted her to the side wall of the hot tub and spread her legs wide. She gasped as cold air hit between her legs, intensifying the pulsing heat that had gripped her there. Jake leaned forward and licked along her slit. Her head fell back, and her fingers dug into the plastic material surrounding the tub. His licks were slow and gentle, applying just enough pressure to her clit to make her squirm for more.

Her hand buried in his hair, trying to pull him closer, but he reached up and tugged it away, placing it back at her side. "Relax, Tessa, and let me lick my fill of you."

She sighed, clenching her fingers at her sides while Jake continued to tongue fuck the life from her. Across the tub, her eyes locked with Mitch's. He didn't say anything, just watched. There was no jealousy, not anger, only love and acceptance. And desire.

The heat emanating from his gaze made her feel even more wanton and sexy. And bold. Never taking her eyes from his, she slid her finger into her mouth, softly sucking at her knuckles. Mitch's eyes narrowed on her lips as she simulated a blowjob. His blue orbs darkened as he watched her, and she moaned around her finger, undulating her hips to the movement of Jake's tongue.

"Damn it," Mitch mumbled. "Fuck her, Jake. Now."

Jake stood and repositioned himself on the seat at the side. Pulling her down, he settled her on his lap, straddling his thick cock.

"Turn her so I can see her," Mitch ordered, and Jake obliged, turning her so that her back was to his chest.

Mitch had moved to settle on the side. His cock stood thick and long against his lower stomach. She licked her lips, wanting to feel his engorged length moving in and out of her mouth, his cum squirting down her throat. Instead, he stayed where he was. His large palm circled his cock and stroked down to his balls as Tessa lifted up and pressed down on Jake's cock.

She gasped loudly as Jake filled her balls deep. His hard length stroked the inside walls of her pussy with the same rhythm Mitch used with his hand. Tessa reached up and squeezed her breasts, her fingers pinching her nipples as she stared at Mitch. This was amazing—fucking Jake in front of

Mitch. He watched her with such love and trust. He made her feel so sexy and so fucking turned on.

Harder she pushed down on Jake, making him groan in pleasure and press upward, filling her even deeper. His relentless cock brushed against her cervix, sending a flutter of pleasure to her womb. "Oh, yes." She sighed and pressed down harder, taking him even deeper.

"Does it feel good, Tess," Mitch asked, his voice strained with lust.

"Yes," she groaned.

"Pinch your nipples for me," Mitch ordered.

Her shaking fingers pinched at her sensitive nipples, then she moved her palms to squeeze at her aching breasts. They felt full and heavy in her hands. Jake's thrusts became faster, harder, and so did Mitch's strokes with his hand. He kept up with them, matching Jake's movements almost perfectly. It was, at times like this, like they were one person.

They moved faster and she groaned, trying to hold off the release she felt skimming just under her flesh. Jake's cock thickened and so did Mitch's. She wanted them to come together. Running her hands down her stomach, she brushed her fingers across her clit. Her hips jerked and the inside of her thighs quivered. Mitch smiled.

"Do it again, Tess."

She did, sighing as she increased the pressure to the swollen nub. Jake's hand joined hers as her body began the upward spiral to fulfillment. Every muscle quaked and she cried out as her body erupted into a massive ball of rapture.

Over and over, her pussy pulsed around Jake's cock, clamping down on his thick length as she pulled him impossibly deeper. With a growl of his own, Jake thrust upward, lifting his hips off the seat as he spilled his seed deep within her body.

Mitch stood and stepped forward, his hand relentlessly pumping his cock. The purple head looked ready to explode, and she reached up to squeeze at his balls. With a shout, Mitch came, shooting cum toward her mouth. Leaning forward, she licked at his cum covered cock, enjoying the salty taste of his juices as they continued to leak out. He moaned, burying his hand in her hair as she licked his shaft clean from balls to tip.

"How's that for an answer, baby?" Jake whispered in her ear.

She moaned, giving Mitch's cock one final suck before sagging back against Jake's panting chest.

"The two of you are going to be the death of me," she whispered in amusement.

Mitch chuckled. "Yeah, but it's a hell of a way to go."

Chapter Fourteen

Mitch checked the safety, then set his gun on the kitchen counter. After what had happened in the Keys, they kept them close by at all times. A snowplow trudged along the mountain road, clearing out a path for traffic. Another hour or so and they'd be able to head down to Gatlinburg for dinner.

The sunshine had already begun to melt the white powder, leaving a thick layer of gray sludge along the edge of the road and sidewalks. It was turning out to be a gorgeous day. But something gnawed at his gut and made him nervous. He'd learned as a SEAL to trust that feeling, and he paid a little more attention to his surroundings than normal.

Adjusting his flannel shirt, Mitch turned to face Jake who stood at the counter making coffee.

"Tessa in the shower?" Mitch asked.

"Yeah. I think that was where she was headed."

Mitch nodded and turned his gaze back out the window. Watching Jake and Tessa earlier in the hot tub had been arousing as hell. She'd looked so beautiful with her flesh flushed in passion, her body undulating against Jake's. There had been no jealousy, no regrets. Only love and desire for a woman he couldn't imagine his life without.

"You all right, Mitch?" Jake asked as he hit the Power button, turning on the coffeepot. The scent of caramel filled the room as it began to brew Tessa's favorite Barnie's coffee.

"Yeah…no," he said with a sigh. "I didn't want to say anything with Tessa down here, but something doesn't feel right."

Jake immediately came to attention and stood straight. "About what?"

"I'm not sure. But I've learned to trust my gut, and my gut says something is about to happen."

Jake nodded and moved to join Mitch at the window. A large black Hummer pulled into the driveway, easily pushing snow out of its way. They glanced at each other with a frown.

"Well, guess your gut was right," Jake said, then moved to grab his pistol from the end table.

Mitch grabbed his from the kitchen counter and slipped it in the waistband at the back of his pants. Glancing back out the window, Mitch noticed Director Sparks climbing from the back of the car, along with Scott Folks, who stepped from the driver side, and a third man neither recognized, but who bore a striking resemblance to Tessa.

"The admiral?" Jake mumbled close to Mitch.

"Possibly. But what the hell are they doing?"

Jake went to open the door and allow the three men inside. "Director. What are you doing here?"

"Jake," he said with a nod of his head as he preceded the other two men into the cabin. "Where's Tessa?"

"She's in the shower," Mitch said.

Sparks nodded and waved a hand toward the tall, older man behind him. "This is Admiral Williams, Tessa's father. Admiral, these are the two men who have been watching over your daughter. Jake Bradley, our computer specialist, and Mitch Robbins, our ex-SEAL."

"Is she all right?" the admiral asked.

He appeared tired and weary. With blue eyes the same as Tessa's, he stared at Mitch expectantly. That feeling in his gut intensified.

"Yes. She's fine," Mitch replied.

"Robbins," the admiral murmured. "You're the one who was hit with armor-piercing rounds in the Middle East. The one who almost died."

"Yes, sir," Mitch said with a frown. "I didn't know my incident was so widely known."

"When bullets pierce our vests the way they did yours, people know about it."

Sparks narrowed his gaze toward Williams in warning, making Mitch frown. What the hell was going on here? Something wasn't right. Jake must have felt it too. He crossed his arms and glared at Sparks.

"What's going on? Did you find the man responsible?"

"You could say that," Sparks said, the corners of his lips lifting in a slight grin.

Mitch caught a movement by the admiral. Using subtle hand signals used by the SEAL teams, he let Mitch know to be on guard. Immediately, Mitch tensed, worry for Tessa gripping his chest.

"Mitch, get Tessa," Sparks ordered. "We need to talk to her."

Mitch's gaze flicked back to the admiral. There was a slight shake of his head, almost unnoticeable, but Mitch caught it and understood. At least he thought he might.

"She's upstairs. I'll be right back."

Turning, he headed up the stairs at a run, toward the master suite. Tessa was just climbing out of the shower. Her hair was damp, her skin sparkling with water droplets. Grabbing a towel off the rack, he tossed it to her, hitting her in the small of the back.

"Dry off quick, Tess," Mitch ordered, then glanced back toward the bedroom door making sure no one had followed him.

"What's going on?" she asked with a frown.

"Sparks is here with your father."

She smiled and began to dry off in earnest. "Daddy's here?"

Brushing past him, she headed toward her clothes lying on the bed. Mitch grabbed her elbow and spun her around to face him. "Listen, Tess. Something's going on. But what, I'm not sure. Just be on guard and do what I tell you without argument. Understand?"

"What's wrong?" she asked, her brow creasing in worry.

"I don't know. Just trust me on this."

"Of course, I trust you."

He cupped her face and smiled down at her. "I love you, Tess," he whispered. "I want you to know that."

"I do know that." She smiled. "What do you think is going to happen, Mitch?"

"I—"

"What the hell is taking you so long?" Scott demanded from the hallway, and Mitch turned to shield Tessa from his view as he stormed into the bedroom.

Tessa gasped and moved to stand close to his back. He reached around, lightly touching her hip in support.

"What the fuck are you doing, Scott? I told you she was taking a shower," Mitch snapped.

"Well, well," Scott drawled, and leaned against the door frame. He crossed his arms over his chest with an arrogant grin, making Mitch grind his teeth in disgust. He'd never liked Scott. The man was an ass.

"Hard to believe someone like the admiral could have a daughter that looks like that. Interesting that she's so comfortable around you naked. Been having a little fun on this job, Mitch?"

"Fuck you," Mitch snarled. "Now get out so she can get dressed."

"Sure," Scott said with a leer. "See you downstairs, gorgeous."

Anger raced through Mitch as he made a move to go after Scott, but Tessa's hand on his wrist stopped him.

"Don't," she whispered. "Who was that?"

"That was General Scott Folks. He's Army and a damn jerk."

Tessa nodded and quickly dressed. Her hands shook slightly as she tried to button her blouse. Mitch stepped over and brushed her hands aside. With a small smile, he finished buttoning it for her.

"Is my dad okay?" she asked.

"Seems to be."

"Good." She sighed.

Giving her hands a gentle squeeze, he handed her a pair of shoes, and then they headed downstairs. Tessa spotted her father immediately and breathed a sigh of relief. He looked so tired, so ragged. She was used to seeing him in his uniform, impeccably dressed and spotless. Not like this. Torn jeans, faded T-shirt, messed-up hair that seemed just a little grayer than before.

"Daddy?" She sighed, then ran down the stairs, throwing herself into his strong, outstretched arms.

"Tessa." He sighed. "Thank God."

Her father held tight, then leaned down to whisper softly in her ear. "It's Sparks. You're in danger."

What?

She pulled back and stared up at him in shock. He brushed his finger over her lips for a brief second, indicating she should be quiet. She nodded and gave him a sideways smile. Her insides began to tighten in knots. Sparks was involved? What did that mean exactly? Were they all in trouble now?

"I think that's enough reunion for you two," Sparks said, then stepped forward and grabbed Tessa's elbow in a punishing grip.

With a jerk, he pulled her aside and spun her around to face her father. Something cold hit the side of her neck, and she stiffened in fear when she realized it was the muzzle of a pistol. Mitch and Jake both tensed in anger, each reaching for his weapon.

"I wouldn't if I were you," Sparks drawled. "Put your guns on the floor and slide them over here."

To her side, Scott also drew a weapon, pointing it at Mitch and Jake. Both men stilled, their gazes jumping back and forth between her and Scott.

"You son of a bitch," Jake snapped as he set his gun on the tile floor, Mitch following suit. "It was you all along?"

"I'm one of many," Sparks drawled. "The codes, Admiral. Now."

"Why? They've already been changed. They were changed the day Tessa went into protective custody," Williams argued back, folding his arms over his chest.

Tessa didn't miss the anguish in his gaze as he watched her, and she swallowed a sob of despair. How were they going to get out of this?

"I don't want those codes," Sparks snarled, tightening his angry hold on Tessa. Her ribs hurt from the pressure of his arm around her middle, and she gasped for any breath of air she could inhale.

"What codes do you want?" Mitch snapped.

"Oh, God," Tessa groaned as she realized what he was asking for. "He wants the access codes to the schematics. Who are you selling the blueprints to?"

"Anybody who wants them. I'm tired of risking my life and running myself ragged for an ungrateful government. I get nothing from them, and I'm taking what I deserve."

"You deserve a stay in a maximum-security prison," Jake snarled.

"Not going to happen," Sparks said with a nasty grin.

"Wanna bet?" Mitch mumbled and took a step back toward the kitchen counter.

His gaze flicked to Tessa's, and she knew immediately what he was about to do. There was a gun hidden in the kitchen drawer. It was the one they'd taken from her in the Keys. Her heart began to pound furiously in her chest as she tried to think of a way to distract them. Anything.

"You know you won't be able to hide from them," Tessa argued, then squealed when he pinched her flesh just below her breast.

Her father stepped forward, until Sparks growled, indicating he should step back.

"I won't have to hide from anyone. As far as NCIS has to know, you were killed by the thieves. I tried to help, but you were already dead when I arrived. The killers got away with access to the blueprints. The military will shut down the project, and I'll keep going, a little heavier in my pocket."

"You're insane," Jake growled.

"No, just pissed and tired of being taken advantage of."

Tessa kept her gaze on Mitch as he crept ever closer to the counter. Even if he got the gun, it would be two against one. The odds of him pulling this off were not good. Fear for Mitch swam through her veins. Fear for all of them.

Glancing to her father, she realized he knew what Mitch was doing, as well. He'd crept closer to her and Sparks, and she didn't miss the subtle messages the two were sending each other. Now that she'd seen it, she realized they were silently communicating. But had Sparks seen it too? She struggled, trying to think of something to do that would distract Sparks and Scott.

Wiggling, she ignored the crushing pain in her ribs and struggled against his tight hold. "Let me go, damn it. We're not giving you anything!"

"Your father will talk now if he doesn't want to see your blood splattered all over his face," Sparks drawled.

Tessa gasped and stomped her foot down on his. "Fuck you!"

Sparks grunted and reached up to pinch at her breast. Hard. Tessa cried out, but couldn't move from his punishing hold on her nipple.

"Stupid bitch," he snarled. "I should shoot you right now, just for the hell of it."

Jake made a move to come at them, but Sparks cocked the gun being held at her throat. "Don't, asshole, or I do it."

Immediately, Jake stopped, his fearful gaze locking with Tessa's. She swallowed hard, trying her best not to cry.

"I love you," she mouthed silently, and Jake nodded, silently mouthing it back to her.

"Oh, isn't that sweet," Scott drawled, and Tessa turned to glare at him. "You must be some kind of woman, Tessa. First I find you upstairs naked with Mitch, and now you're whispering sweet words of love to Jake."

"She was getting out of the shower, you ass," Mitch snarled from behind the counter.

He'd made it to the drawer, but would he be able to get it open without them realizing it?

"All right," her father shouted. "I'll give you the code, but I want Tessa by my side first."

Sparks snorted. "No."

It was all Mitch needed. Tessa watched from the corner of her eye as his hand slid stealthily into the drawer and pulled out the gun. Every muscle in her body tensed as the action began to unfold in slow motion around her. Mitch fired, hitting Scott, but not before Scott fired, sending Mitch flying backward as a bullet ripped through his stomach. Tessa screamed for Mitch as her father rushed forward and grabbed Sparks's hand that held the gun.

Sparks had to let her go in order to fight with her father. The second his grip loosened, Jake shoved her out of the way, knocking her to the floor. With a sob, she crawled forward toward Mitch's still form lying just a few feet away. She tried not to look at Scott's dead body, his chest open and seeping blood. The scent of death and gun smoke filled her lungs, making her gag. The distance seemed to go on forever as Jake and her father struggled with Sparks.

The shot startled her and she stopped, turning with dread to see who'd been shot. Sparks's eyes widened with shock, and he fell to his knees, his hands grasping the seeping hole in his chest. His gaze locked with hers as he fell forward, the air gurgling from his lungs.

Mitch groaned, drawing her attention from Sparks, and she stumbled to her feet, trying to get to him. "Mitch," she cried as she dropped to her knees by his stomach.

The bullet had hit his side, but there was so much blood. Her hands shook as she opened his shirt, allowing her to see the wound. "I need a towel, a shirt…something to stop the bleeding," she shouted as she pressed down on the wound with her palm.

Mitch grunted and opened his eyes. "Damn, that hurts," he groaned.

"What were you thinking?" She sighed, relief sending tears streaming down her cheeks. At least he was alive and the wound didn't appear to be life threatening.

He shrugged, then winced at the movement. "I've already been shot six times. What's one more bullet?"

"Oh, Mitch." She sighed, then grinned. "Ever the comedian."

"Anything to see you smile," he whispered, then closed his eyes.

Tessa thought he'd passed out, but he shifted, trying to find a more comfortable position. He grunted in pain, his face scrunching up.

"Be still, Mitch," Jake ordered from behind Tessa. "I've called an ambulance and they're on the way."

"Who…" Mitch swallowed, then tried again. "We need to find out who else was involved."

"I have a few names, one of which is Korean."

"We may have killed the Korean in the Keys, as well as one more," Jake said.

"Actually," Mitch mumbled. "Tessa killed the Korean."

"Be quiet," she and Jake ordered at the same time.

* * *

Mitch sighed as he glanced around his stark white hospital room. He'd been here for three days and was bored out of his mind. If he didn't get out of this room soon, he'd go stark raving mad.

Jake had worked with Tessa's father, going through hours of grilling questions from NCIS and JAG officials.

Tessa had remained by his side, taking care of him and making sure he had whatever he needed. She was his angel, and for the last day and a half all he could think about was sinking between her beautiful thighs. Even shot and in pain, he wanted her.

"God help me." He sighed toward the ceiling.

"God help you with what?" she asked in amusement as the door to his room shut behind her. Her hair was pulled back in a French braid. Pearl earrings dangled from her ears. The black slacks and white shirt made her appear innocent and conservative. He almost snorted at the conservative image. His Tessa was as wild and willing as they came.

Smiling down at him, she placed another delivery of flowers by his bed.

"God help me if I have to look at another vase of flowers."

Tessa laughed. "You're a popular guy. Enjoy it."

As she brushed by, he grabbed her wrist and pulled her down on the bed next to him. "How are you doing, Tess?" he asked.

"I'm fine," she said with a smile. "Much better now that I know you'll be back to your normal self in no time."

Mitch smiled and softly touched the side of her face. "I'm a tough bird to get rid of. I love you, Tess," he whispered.

"I love you too."

"Have you talked to your dad?"

Tessa sighed and glanced down at her hands clasped on her thigh. "Only about what's going on with the agency. Not about you and Jake."

"You don't have to."

"I know. But I know if I don't tell him, he'll realize something isn't quite right. I mean, look how I handled this whole you getting shot thing. He knows I have feelings for you, and he also knows I told Jake I love him." With a sigh, she glanced up toward the ceiling. "He'll never understand."

"You should have a little more faith in me, Tessa."

Tessa jerked around and stared, wide-eyed, at her father standing in the doorway. He was back in his uniform, his hair cut and properly groomed. This was the father she knew.

Jake was behind him, his smile wide and full of love. "I talked to your father," Jake said.

"You what?" She gulped, her face heating in embarrassment.

"It's okay, Tessa. I may have some adjusting to do, but if this is what you want, I know the two of them love you and will do whatever they can to make you happy."

She didn't speak. She couldn't. She could only stare at her father in stunned silence. Jake had talked to him? Mitch shoved at her lightly, and she turned to look at him. He smiled, inclining his head toward her father. "Go to him," he whispered.

He was right. It had probably taken a lot for her father to do this. To try and understand. She stood and walked toward him, wrapping her arms around his neck.

Her father held tight, sighing into her neck. "I love you, Tessa. You're all I have left of your mother, and I don't want to lose you too. Not over something as trivial as this."

Tears streamed down her face as she fought hard not to sob out loud. For a man who had a hard time showing emotion, it was the most he'd opened up to her in a long time. "I love you too, Daddy," she whispered.

"I have another confession to make," Jake said from his stance at the doorway. She pulled away from her dad and stared at him.

"What?" she asked.

"Well, not really a confession, but an apology. I was wrong about Kate." Opening the door, he smiled as Kate stepped into the room.

Tessa squealed and ran to embrace her friend in a huge hug. Kate hugged her back with a laugh.

"I'm so glad you're okay," Kate said.

"I always knew you couldn't have had anything to do with this."

"Jake told me what he thought." Leaning closer, Kate whispered. "You are so damn lucky. When we're alone you have to tell me what being with two men is like."

Tessa laughed at her friend. Kate would never change, and Tessa wouldn't have it any other way.

Epilogue

Tessa stood between Jake and Mitch on the soft sands of the Caribbean beach. The warm sun slipped below the horizon, casting the clouds in shades of red and gold. The tropical breeze blew, bringing with it the scent of ocean and tropical flowers and whipping her white lace dress around her ankles.

Jake and Mitch both looked incredible in navy blue Dockers and white shirts. They wore them open to halfway down their chest. The white was a stark contrast to their dark tans. Jake's longer hair blew in the slight breeze, while Mitch's short, cropped locks remained firmly in place. The sunlight highlighted the gray streaks and she reached up to touch one with a smile. Mitch hated the gray. He'd always said, he might grow old, but he'd never grow up. Mitch was more grown-up than he would admit. He just liked acting the nut.

Behind her stood Kate and her father as she exchanged vows with Jake officially, then Mitch unofficially. The two slipped a ring on her finger together. It was a one-karat diamond with an emerald on each side, just a little smaller. The diamond represented her, always surrounded and protected by the emeralds. It was a beautiful ring and an even more beautiful sentiment. Just like her bracelet, which she'd worn every day since Mitch had given it to her.

Her life couldn't be any better.

Once the ceremony was over, Kate and her father came up to hug her, wishing her happiness. Her father even shook Jake's and Mitch's hands, finally giving his approval to the union, before they headed to the yacht Jake had reserved for their honeymoon.

But Tessa had one surprise she hadn't shared yet. She was pregnant. But whose baby it would be, she had no idea. Maybe it was fate's way of telling them they didn't need to know. She'd been on the Pill, but didn't even realize until days later that she'd left the pills in the Keys, completely forgetting them in her haste and nervousness.

She remained tense until the yacht pulled away from the dock. For two weeks they'd travel from one island to another, sightseeing and shopping. It was a honeymoon she looked forward to. But what she looked forward to the most was the time alone with her two husbands. Well, alone except for the small crew taking care of the boat.

Worried about how they would take the news of her pregnancy, she steeled her spine. With a deep breath for courage, she joined Mitch and Jake in the living room. Large windows provided a beautiful view of the water and moonlight glistening on the waves. Mitch stood at the bar, his shirt hanging out of his pants, the buttons undone. With the view of that trim waist and amazing chest, she almost forgot what she wanted to tell them. Jake sat on the couch, his shirt also undone and his arm lying along the back. In his hand was a cup of steaming coffee.

"Hey, beautiful," Mitch said with a grin, and she returned his smile with a hesitant one.

"Is something wrong, Tessa?" Jake asked as he watched her in concern.

They always seemed to know when she was upset or worried. It was at times unnerving, and at others, so comforting.

"Not wrong, really." She sighed. "I'm just not sure how you guys are going to take it."

"Take what, baby?" Jake asked.

"I told you when we were in the Keys that I was on the Pill."

"You lied so you could trap us," Mitch teased, but when she didn't deny it, his smile faded.

"I didn't lie," she started. "I was on them at the time, but when we left, I forgot them and didn't realize it right away."

"Tessa," Jake began as he set his cup on the glass coffee table. "Are you trying to tell us you're pregnant?"

"Yes." She wrung her hands in front of her. "And I don't know which of you is the father."

She watched them, her heart skipping in her chest wildly. They turned to each other, the shock evident on their faces. Would they be happy? Upset? Would they demand to know which one of them had fathered the child?

"I know it's not the way it was supposed to happen, but we can do DNA testing to see who the father is. I want the baby, guys."

Jake frowned and stood, stepping toward her. "Tessa…" He stopped and covered his mouth with his palm. Dropping to his knees, he kissed her stomach, laying his forehead against her. Mitch walked over and placed a soft kiss on her cheek, his eyes smiling in happiness.

"You guys are okay?" she asked.

Jake grabbed her hands and tugged her to her knees. Cupping her cheeks, he smiled at her. "More than okay. You know what? I don't think it matters who is really the father."

"I agree," Mitch said as he settled on his knees next to her. "It will be both of ours. A baby we all created together."

A tear slipped from the corner of her eye and slid down her cheek. She sighed in relief and quickly kissed each of them. "I love you both, so much."

"We love you too, baby," Jake whispered and placed his hand over her stomach. "I'm afraid to touch you now."

Tessa laughed. "You better get over that real quick, mister. Because it's my honeymoon and I want to be made love to. By both of you."

Jake and Mitch both smiled.

"Gently," Jake whispered as he placed soft, featherlight kisses along her jaw.

"And very slowly," Mitch said as he nipped just behind her ear.

She shivered in anticipation. She could handle gently and slowly. Most definitely.

THE END

Trista Ann Michaels

Trista lives in the land of dreams, where alpha men are tender and heroines are strong and sassy. When not there, she visits the mountains of Tennessee. Not a bad place to spend a little spare time when she needs a break from all those voices in her head. Unfortunately they never fail to find her.